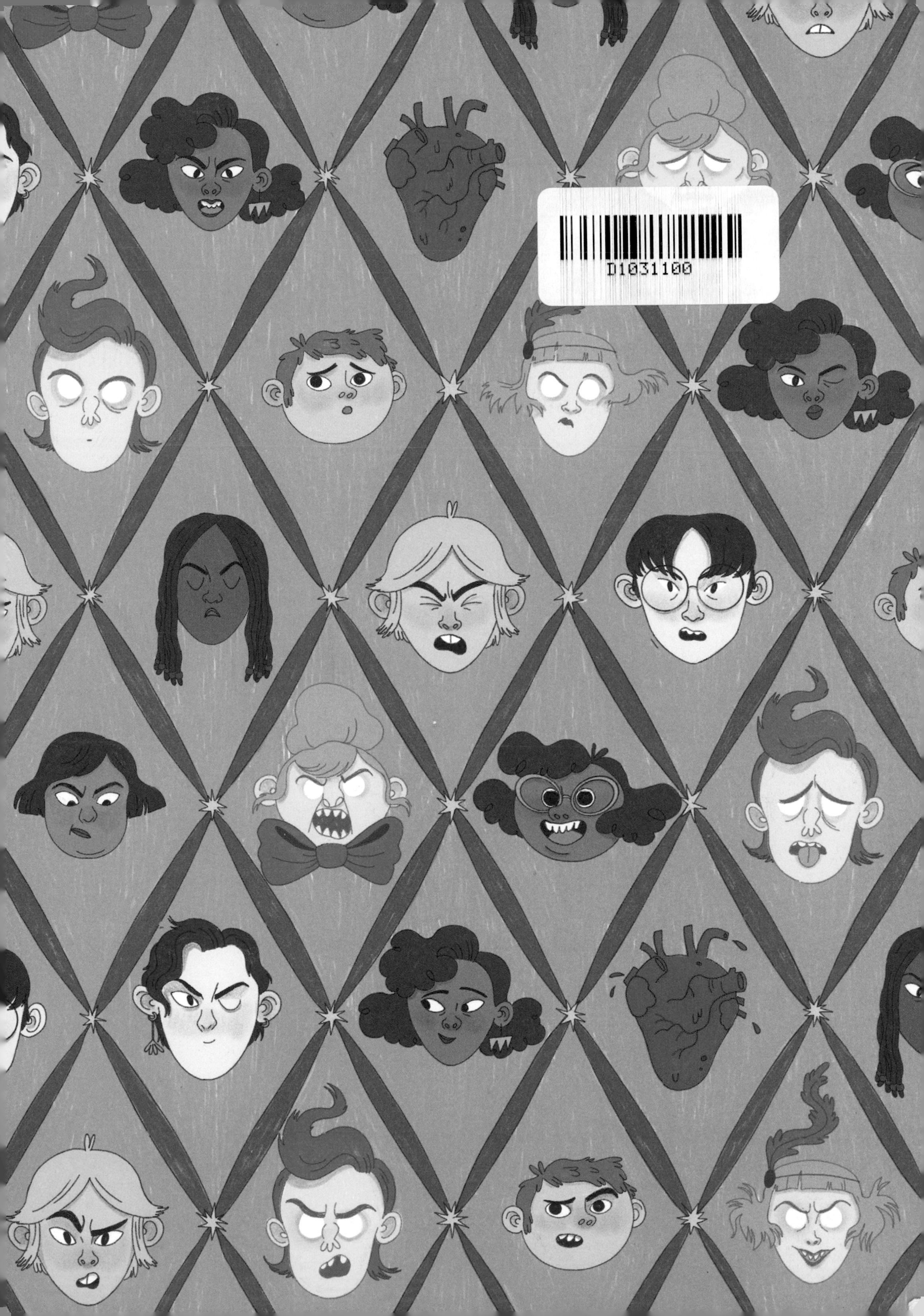

THIS BOOK IS FOR
~WOMSIE~

MOST OF THE TOAST
BEST IN THE WEST

SMELLY

7-9ft

furry—

Remember to call Nana!

Mason Mooney: Paranormal Investigator © Flying Eye Books 2020.

First edition published in 2020 by Flying Eye Books,
an imprint of Nobrow Ltd. 27 Westgate Street, London, E8 3RL.

Text and illustrations © Seaerra Miller 2020

Seaerra Miller has asserted her right under the Copyright, Designs and Patents Act, 1988, to be identified as
the Author and Illustrator of this Work.

1 3 5 7 9 10 8 6 4 2

Published in the US by Nobrow (US) Inc.

Printed in Poland on FSC® certified paper.

ISBN: 978-1-912497-64-5

FSC
www.fsc.org
MIX
Paper from
responsible sources
FSC® C001693

www.flyingeyebooks.com

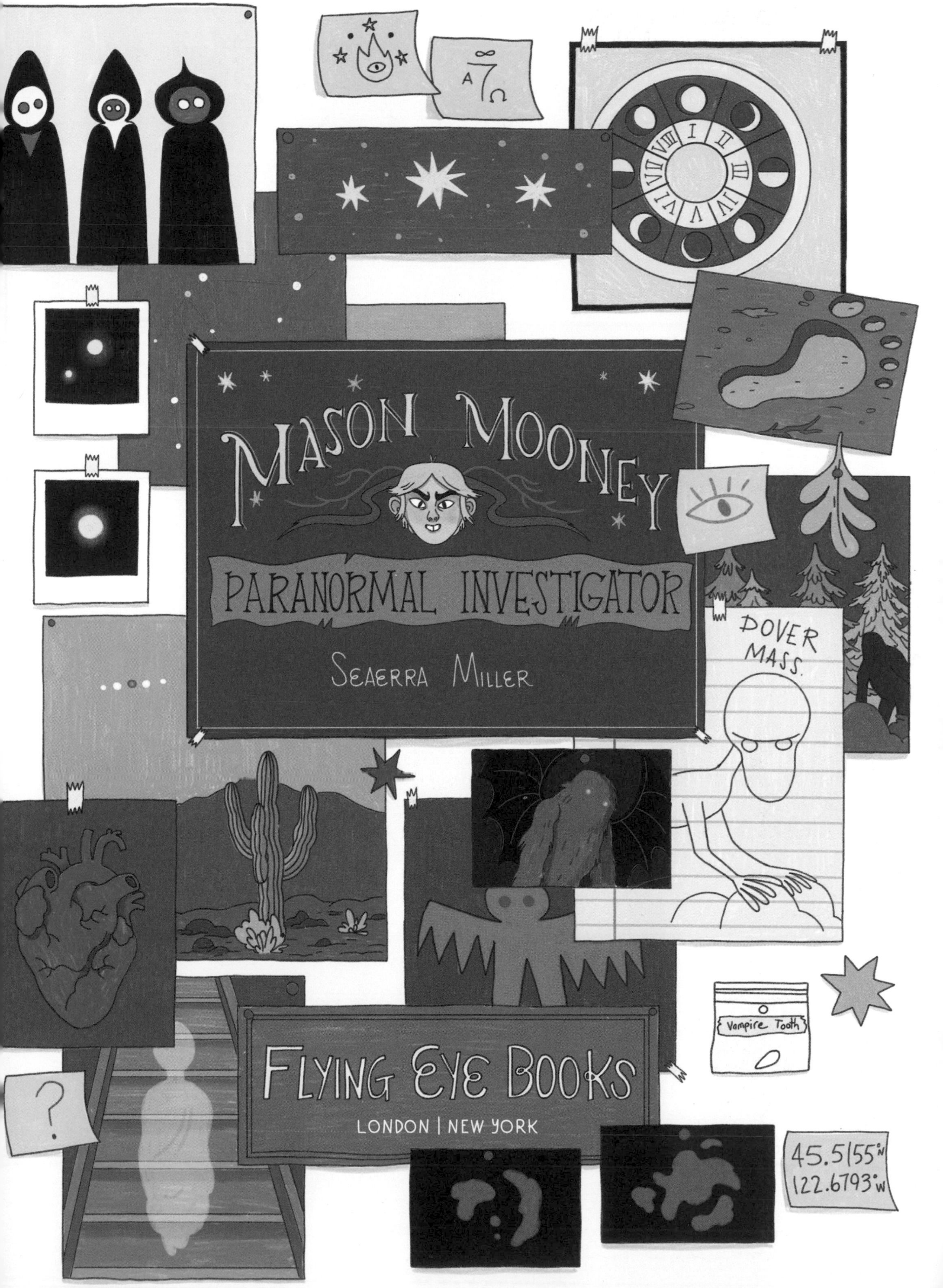
MASON MOONEY
PARANORMAL INVESTIGATOR
SEAERRA MILLER
DOVER MASS.
Vampire Tooth
?
FLYING EYE BOOKS
LONDON | NEW YORK
45.5155°N
122.6793°W

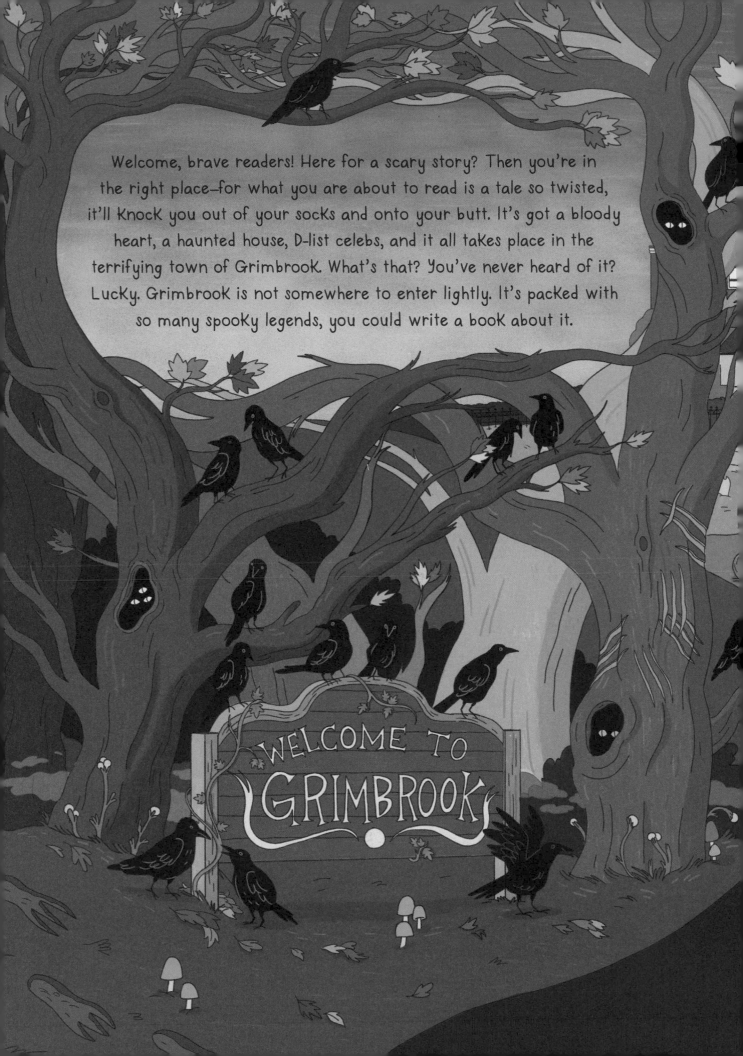

Welcome, brave readers! Here for a scary story? Then you're in the right place—for what you are about to read is a tale so twisted, it'll knock you out of your socks and onto your butt. It's got a bloody heart, a haunted house, D-list celebs, and it all takes place in the terrifying town of Grimbrook. What's that? You've never heard of it? Lucky. Grimbrook is not somewhere to enter lightly. It's packed with so many spooky legends, you could write a book about it.

WELCOME TO GRIMBROOK

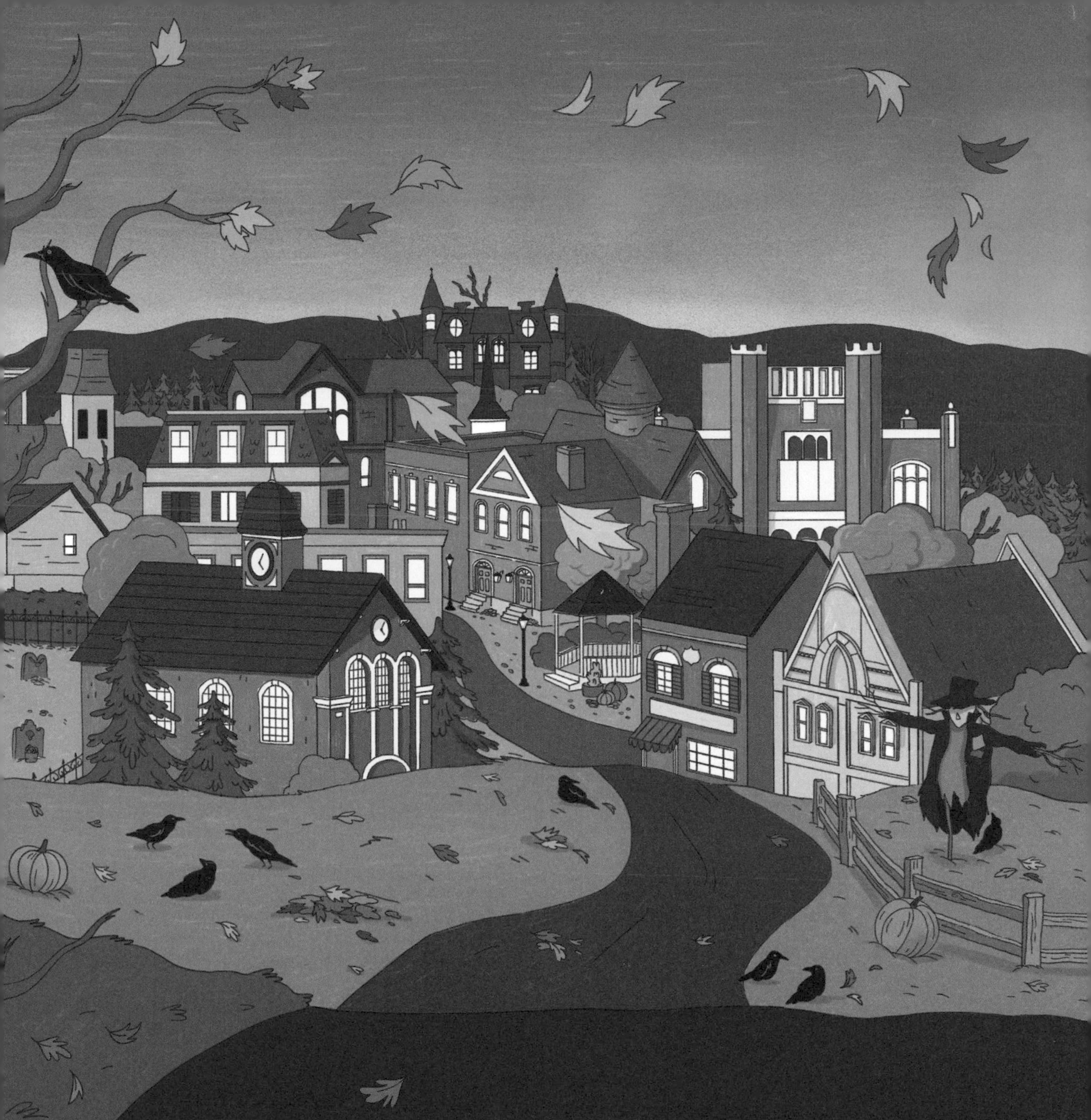

Some say it's because the town falls on an electromagnetic ley line. Others believe it's been cursed by an evil witch. Mostly people just say the legends are hooey and try to ignore the unexplained shadows they see in the corners of their eyes . . . or the mysterious footprints in the woods. But there's one person in Grimbrook who's made it his mission to get to the bottom of these freaky phenomena. This is the story of Mason Mooney and the odd goings-on he seems to encounter on a daily basis. Perhaps you've heard of him? No? He's super famous . . . or so he keeps saying. Really? You've never heard of him? Well then, get ready, 'cause here's the scoop. . . .

Mason Mooney is an aspiring paranormal investigator. For as long as he can remember, he's been obsessed with the unexplained. He's made it his mission to get to the bottom of Grimbrook's most mysterious mysteries. He's always busy ordering haunted objects off the Internet or sticking his nose in some smelly old book.

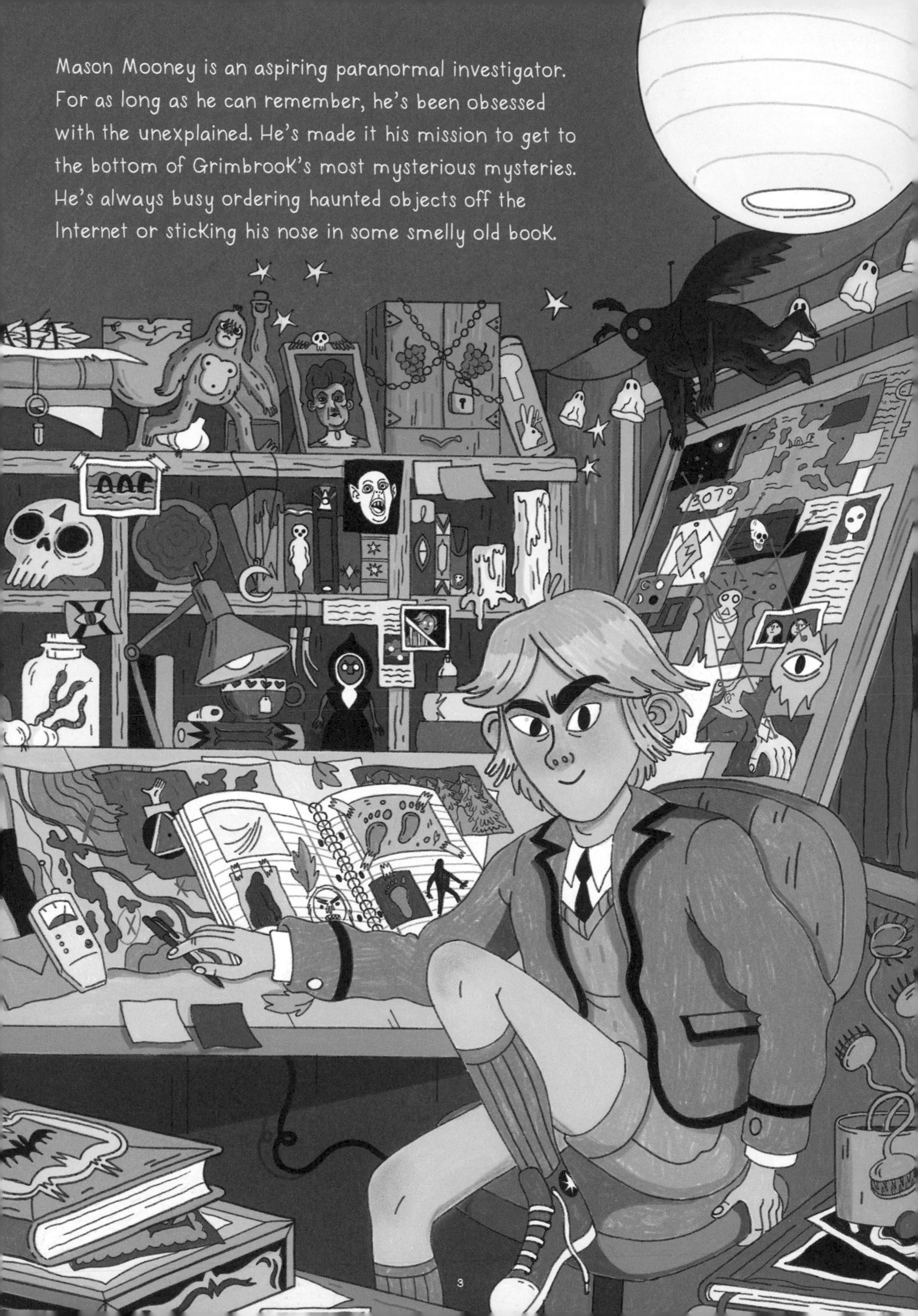

He even claims to have had a few close run-ins with Grimbrook's elusive creatures. Trust me, he's only too happy to tell anyone who'll listen about—

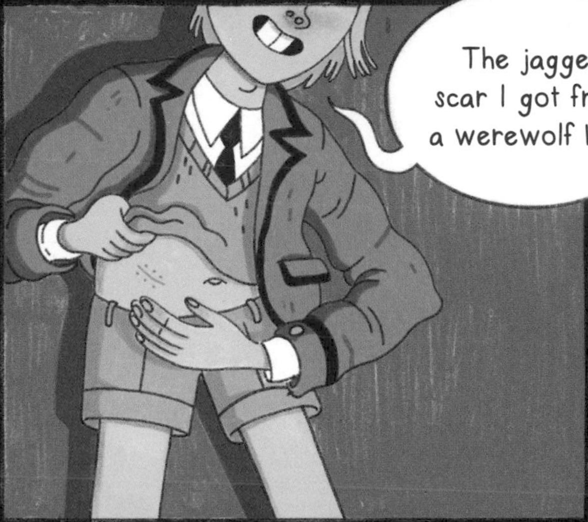
The jagged scar I got from a werewolf bite.

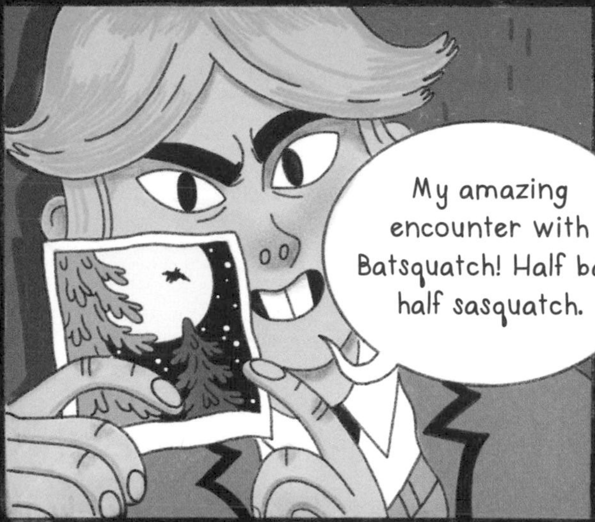
My amazing encounter with Batsquatch! Half bat, half sasquatch.

You could say that Mason is something of a mystery himself. After all, it's not every day you meet someone who carries around a live, beating heart in a jar. He's a bit stingy with the details on how that came to be. All I know is that it has something to do with a Death Worm and some legal technicalities. But I'm getting ahead of myself.

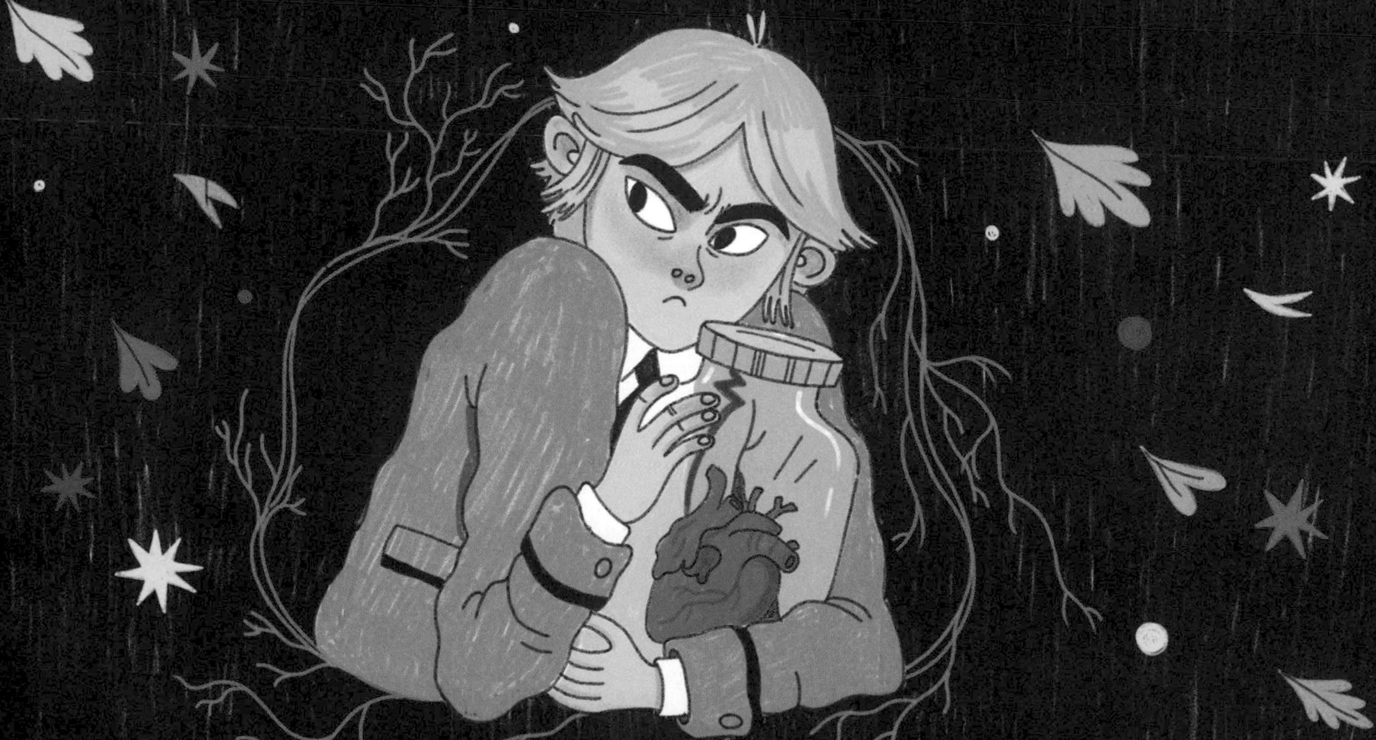

Sit your butt down and keep the lights ON. This is going to get creepy. I mean, I guess they'd have to be on anyway because you're reading a book, but just double check, OK? Here goes. . . . This story starts with a letter.

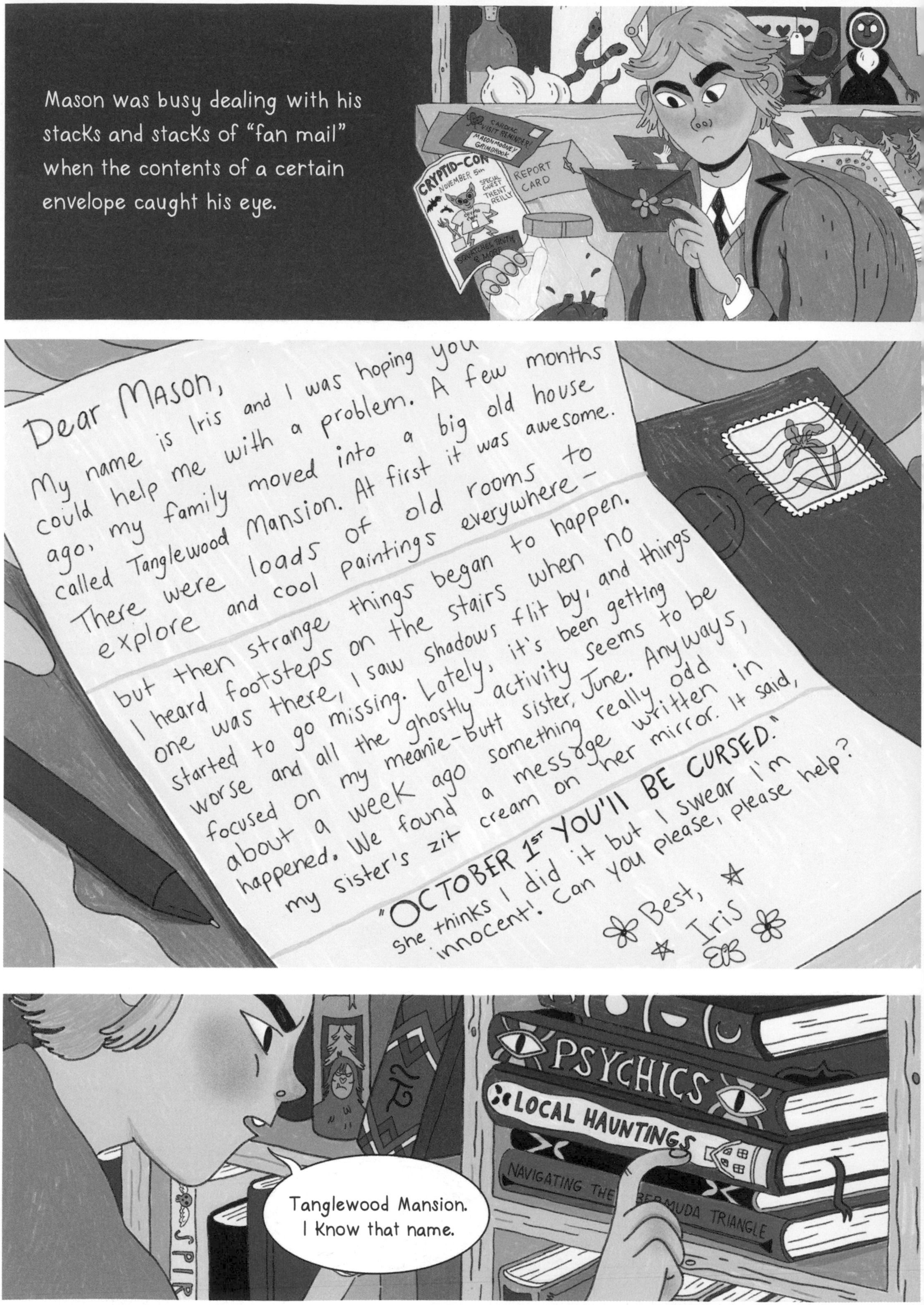
Mason was busy dealing with his stacks and stacks of "fan mail" when the contents of a certain envelope caught his eye.
CRYPTID-CON
REPORT CARD
Dear Mason,
My name is Iris and I was hoping you could help me with a problem. A few months ago, my family moved into a big old house called Tanglewood Mansion. At first it was awesome. There were loads of old rooms to explore and cool paintings everywhere –
but then strange things began to happen. I heard footsteps on the stairs when no one was there, I saw shadows flit by, and things started to go missing. Lately, it's been getting worse and all the ghostly activity seems to be focused on my meanie-butt sister, June. Anyways, about a week ago something really odd happened. We found a message written in my sister's zit cream on her mirror. It said,
"OCTOBER 1ST YOU'll BE CURSED."
She thinks I did it but I swear I'm innocent! Can you please, please help?
Best,
Iris
PSYCHICS
LOCAL HAUNTINGS
NAVIGATING THE
TRIANGLE
Tanglewood Mansion. I know that name.

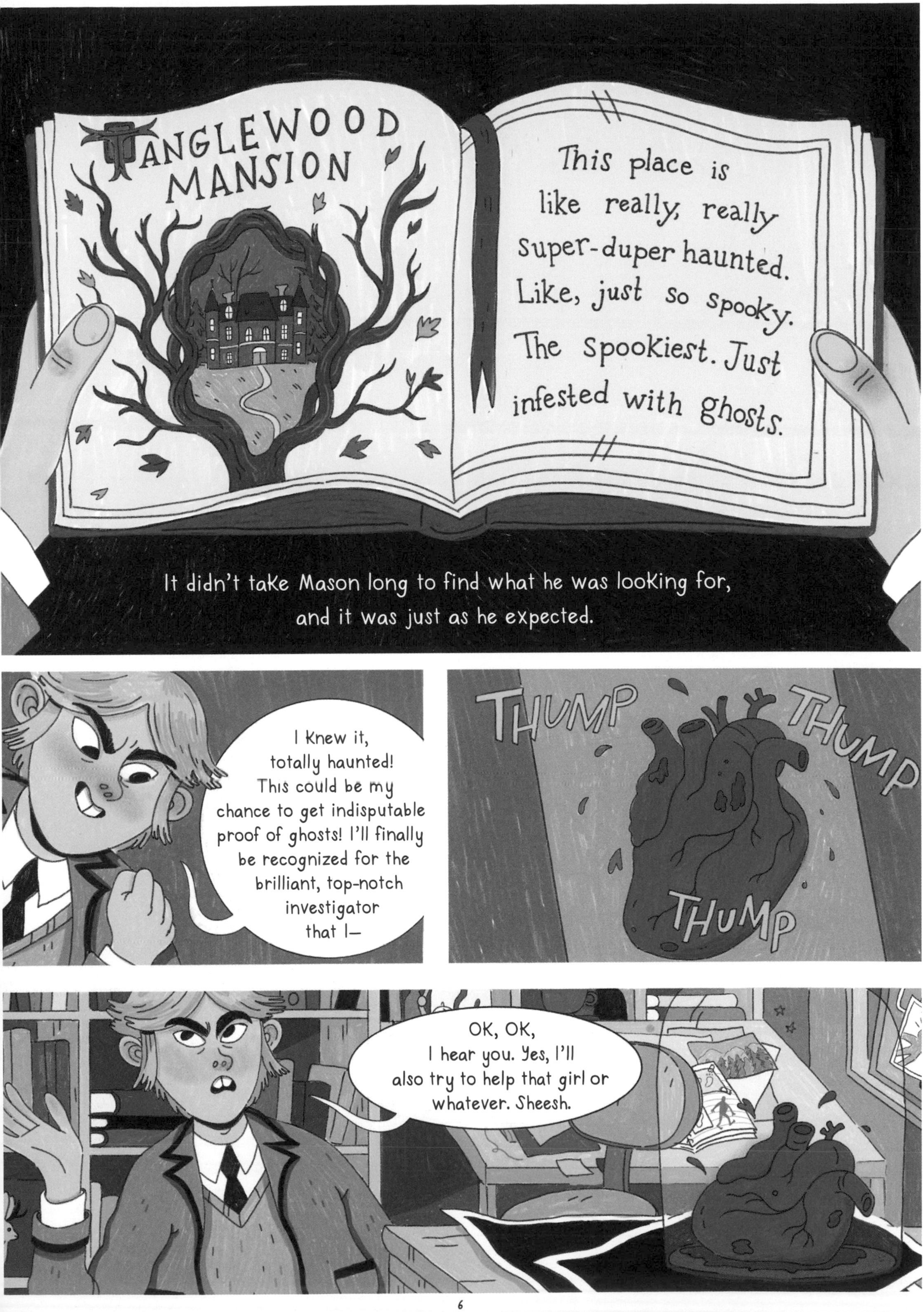
TANGLEWOOD MANSION
This place is like really, really super-duper haunted. Like, just so spooky. The spookiest. Just infested with ghosts.
It didn't take Mason long to find what he was looking for, and it was just as he expected.
I knew it, totally haunted! This could be my chance to get indisputable proof of ghosts! I'll finally be recognized for the brilliant, top-notch investigator that I—
THUMP THUMP THUMP
OK, OK, I hear you. Yes, I'll also try to help that girl or whatever. Sheesh.

So, on the allegedly fateful morning of October first, Mason packed up his investigative supplies and set off for Tanglewood Mansion. It was pretty clear to Mason even before he'd reached the door, that something funky-weird was going on in this house. Mason could feel it in his very bones.

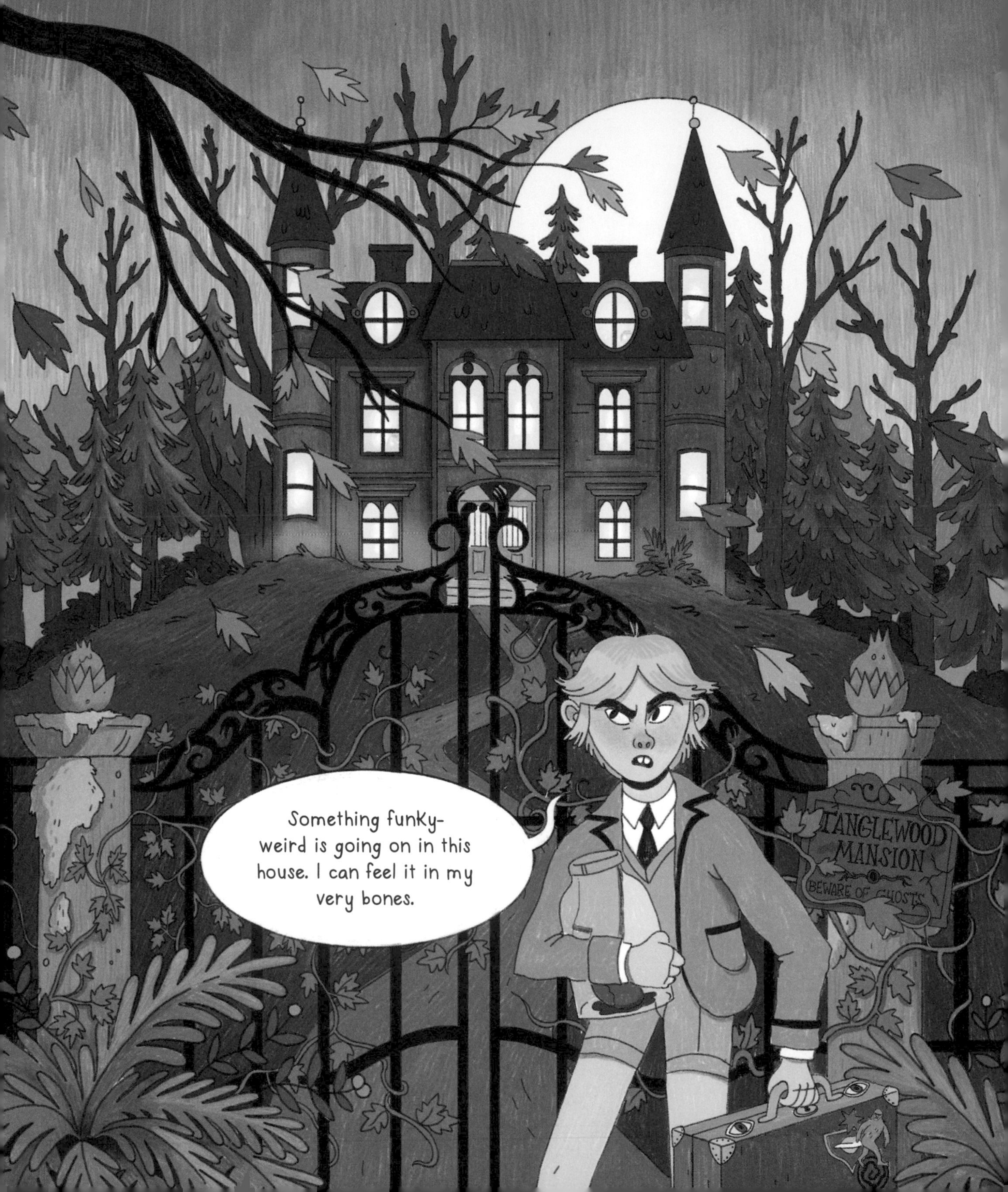
Something funky-weird is going on in this house. I can feel it in my very bones.
TANGLEWOOD MANSION
BEWARE OF GHOSTS

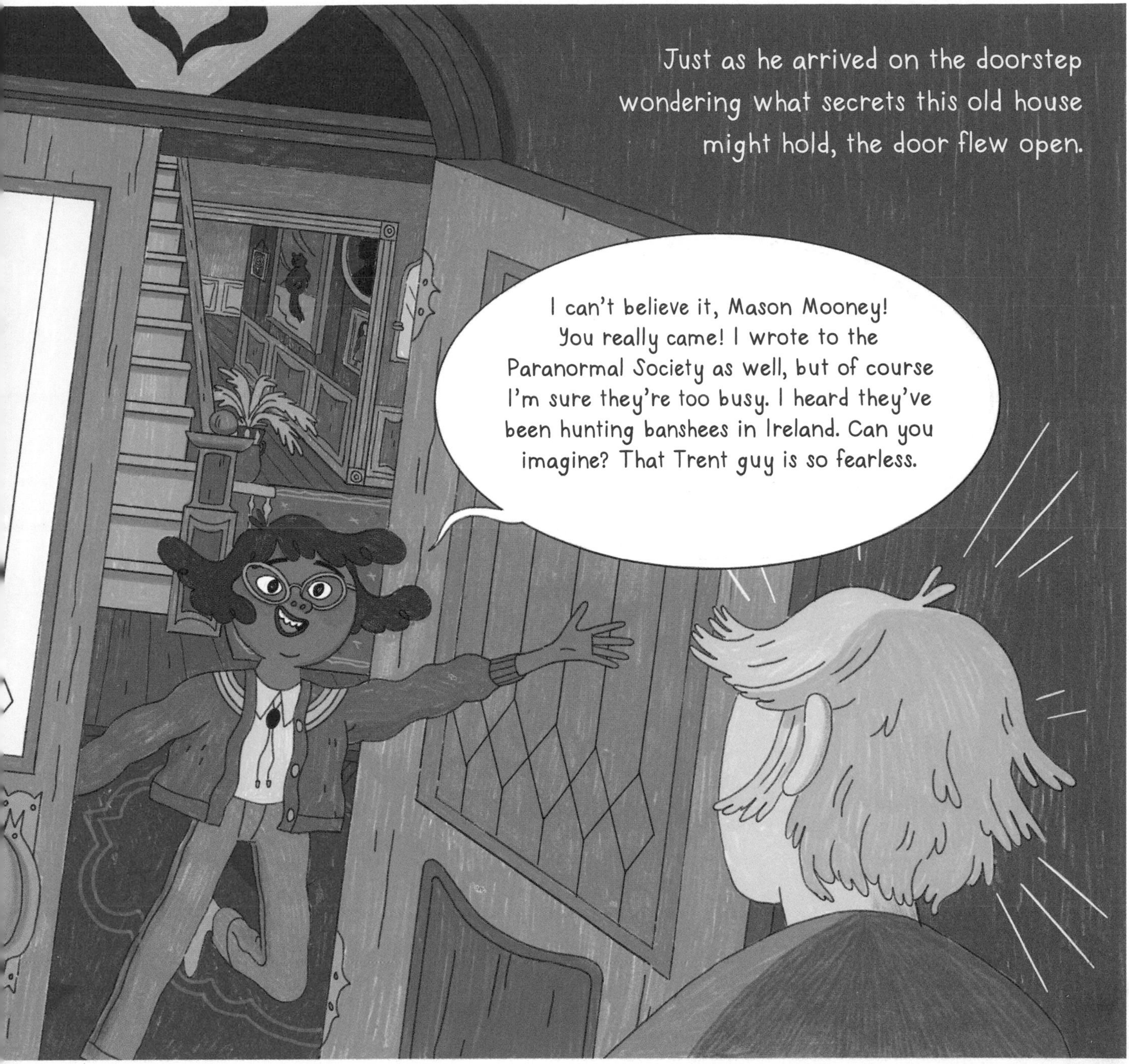
Just as he arrived on the doorstep wondering what secrets this old house might hold, the door flew open.
I can't believe it, Mason Mooney! You really came! I wrote to the Paranormal Society as well, but of course I'm sure they're too busy. I heard they've been hunting banshees in Ireland. Can you imagine? That Trent guy is so fearless.

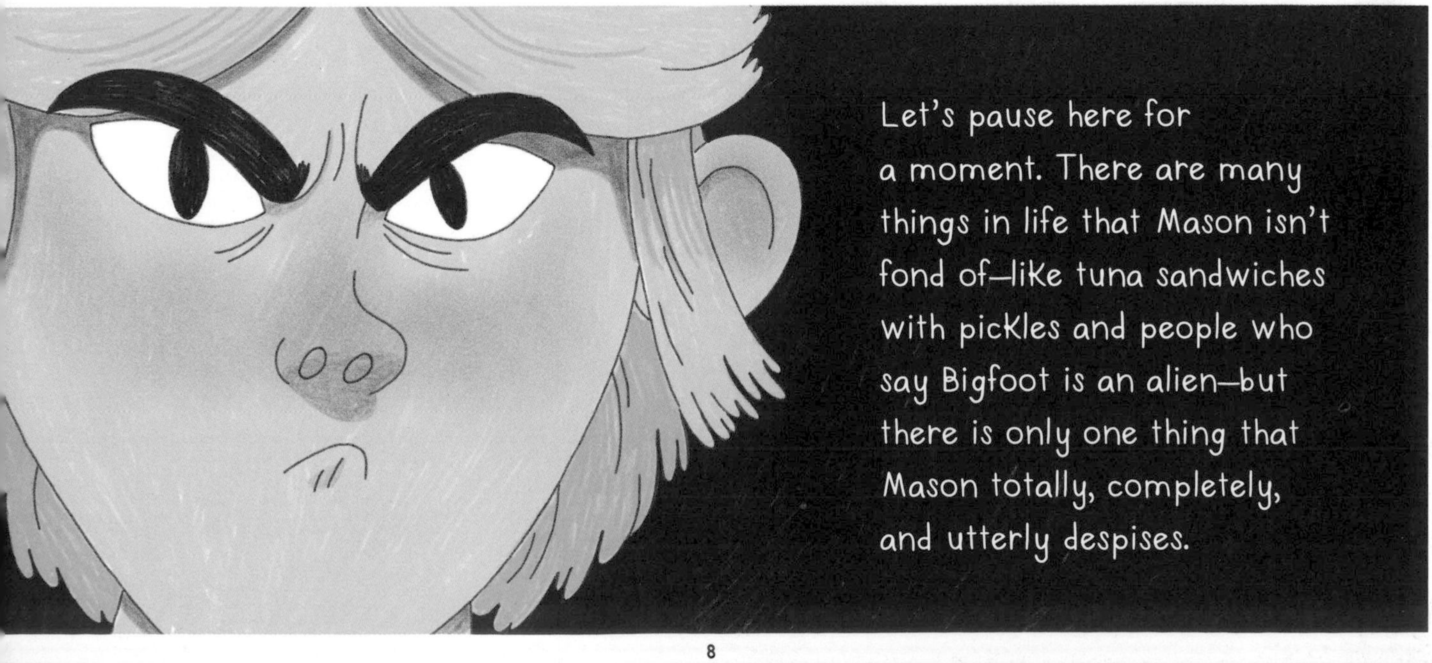
Let's pause here for a moment. There are many things in life that Mason isn't fond of—like tuna sandwiches with pickles and people who say Bigfoot is an alien—but there is only one thing that Mason totally, completely, and utterly despises.

The PARANORMAL Society

Grimbrook's very own team of paranormal investigators, led by heartthrob Trent Reilly, are the hippest kids in town. Originally the cast of a viral video, this group was catapulted into stardom quicker than you can say Loch Ness Monster.

The team now travels the globe seeking out the unknown for their hugely popular TV show, *Trent's Creepy Cases*.

They even have a line of paranormal investigation kits and apparel on the market.

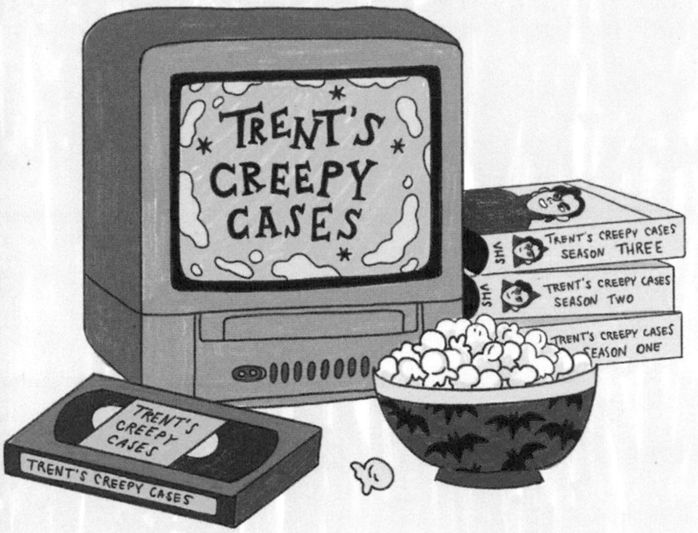
TRENT'S CREEPY CASES
TRENT'S CREEPY CASES SEASON THREE
TRENT'S CREEPY CASES SEASON TWO
TRENT'S CREEPY CASES
VHS
VHS
VHS
TRENT'S CREEPY CASES
TRENT'S CREEPY CASES

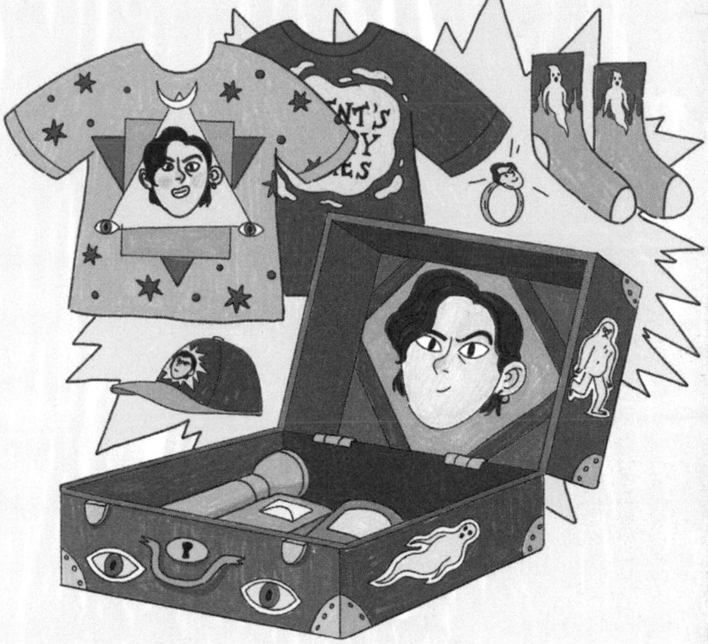

If that wasn't enough, you can pick up Trent's memoir *Sixteen Years: My Life with Ghouls, Gremlins, and Acne*. I won't lie, I cried reading it. To see someone so handsome overcome that zit, well, it was touching. I mean, I know I'm the narrator and I'm only supposed to narrate, but seriously, this guy has got it.

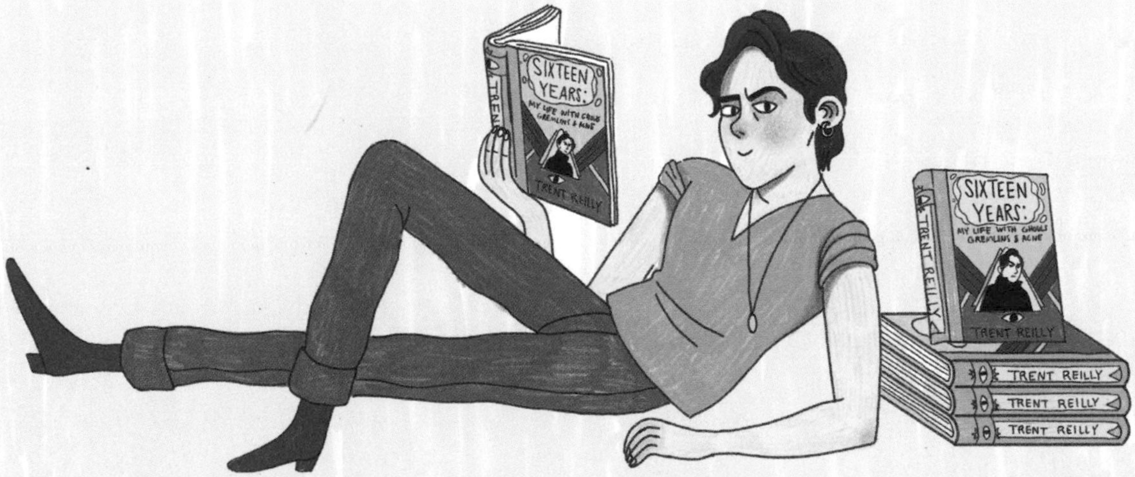
SIXTEEN YEARS:
TRENT REILLY
SIXTEEN YEARS:
MY LIFE WITH GHOULS GREMLINS & ACNE
TRENT REILLY
TRENT REILLY
TRENT REILLY
TRENT REILLY
TRENT REILLY

Anyway, I'm rambling. What I'm trying to say is that Mason didn't exactly like the society. He kind of despised them. So as you can guess, Iris wasn't really making the best first impression.

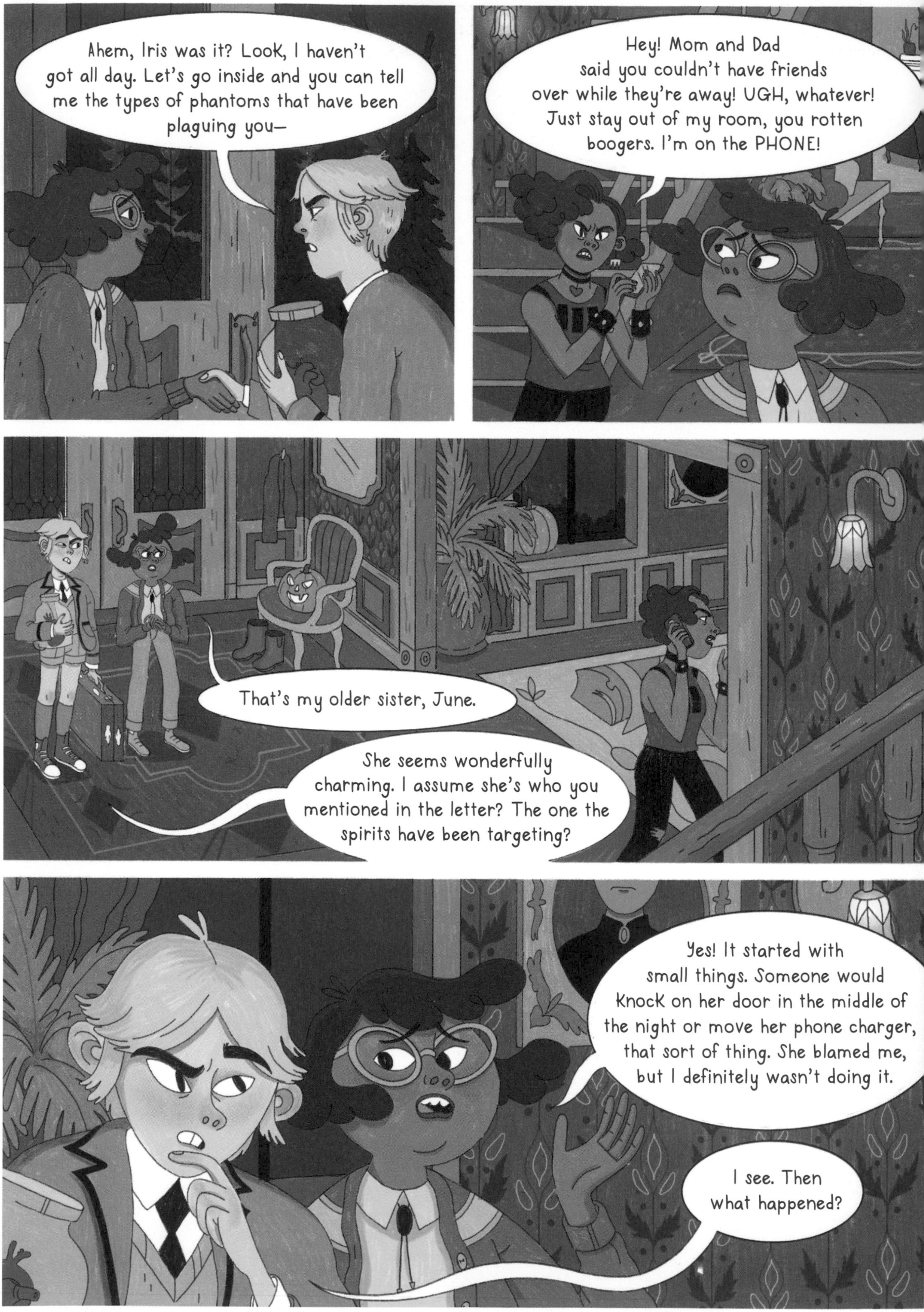
Ahem, Iris was it? Look, I haven't got all day. Let's go inside and you can tell me the types of phantoms that have been plaguing you—
Hey! Mom and Dad said you couldn't have friends over while they're away! UGH, whatever! Just stay out of my room, you rotten boogers. I'm on the PHONE!
That's my older sister, June.
She seems wonderfully charming. I assume she's who you mentioned in the letter? The one the spirits have been targeting?
Yes! It started with small things. Someone would knock on her door in the middle of the night or move her phone charger, that sort of thing. She blamed me, but I definitely wasn't doing it.
I see. Then what happened?

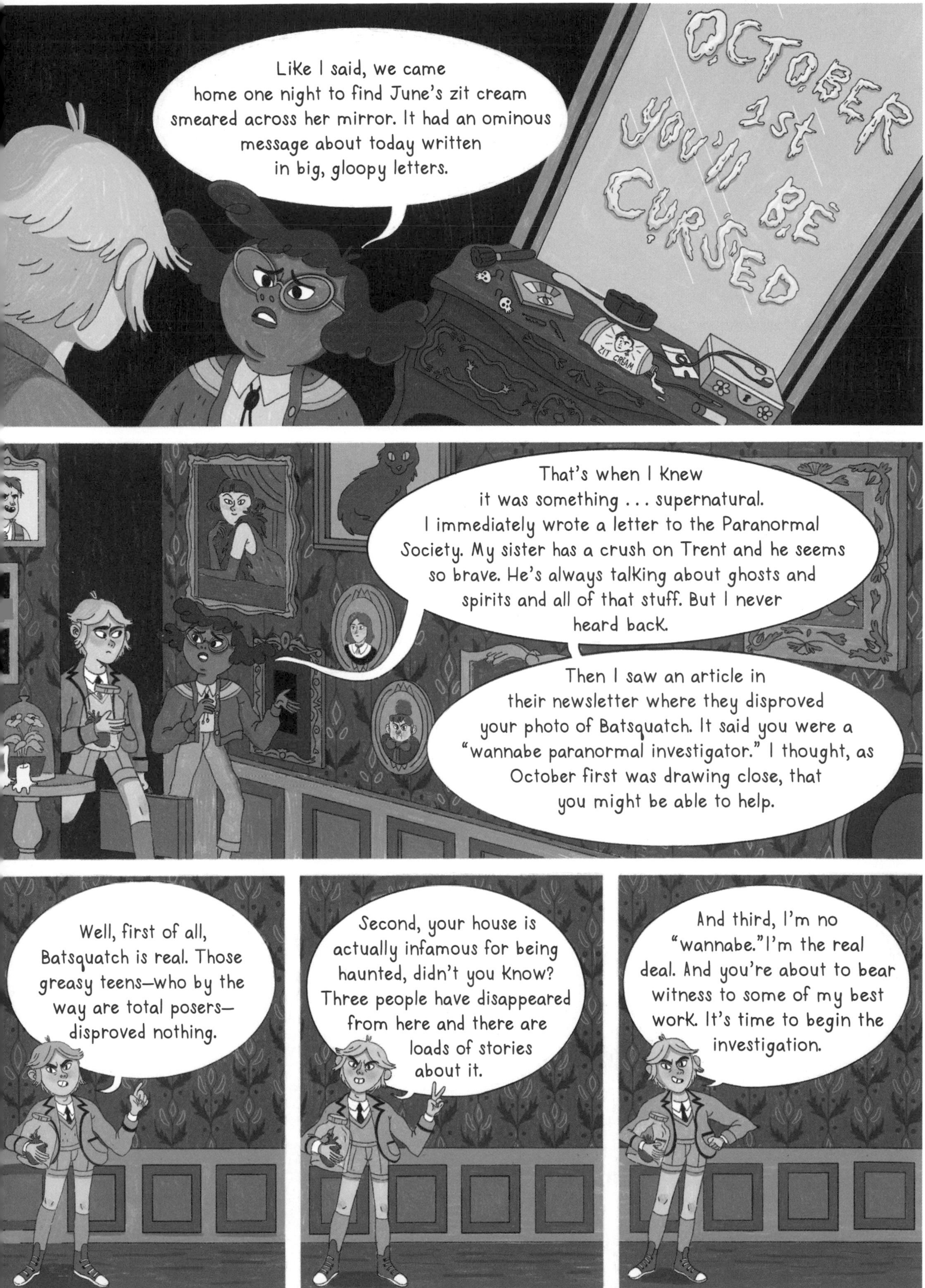
Like I said, we came home one night to find June's zit cream smeared across her mirror. It had an ominous message about today written in big, gloopy letters.
OCTOBER 1st YOU'll BE CURSED
ZIT CREAM
That's when I knew it was something . . . supernatural. I immediately wrote a letter to the Paranormal Society. My sister has a crush on Trent and he seems so brave. He's always talking about ghosts and spirits and all of that stuff. But I never heard back.
Then I saw an article in their newsletter where they disproved your photo of Batsquatch. It said you were a "wannabe paranormal investigator." I thought, as October first was drawing close, that you might be able to help.
Well, first of all, Batsquatch is real. Those greasy teens—who by the way are total posers—disproved nothing.
Second, your house is actually infamous for being haunted, didn't you know? Three people have disappeared from here and there are loads of stories about it.
And third, I'm no "wannabe." I'm the real deal. And you're about to bear witness to some of my best work. It's time to begin the investigation.

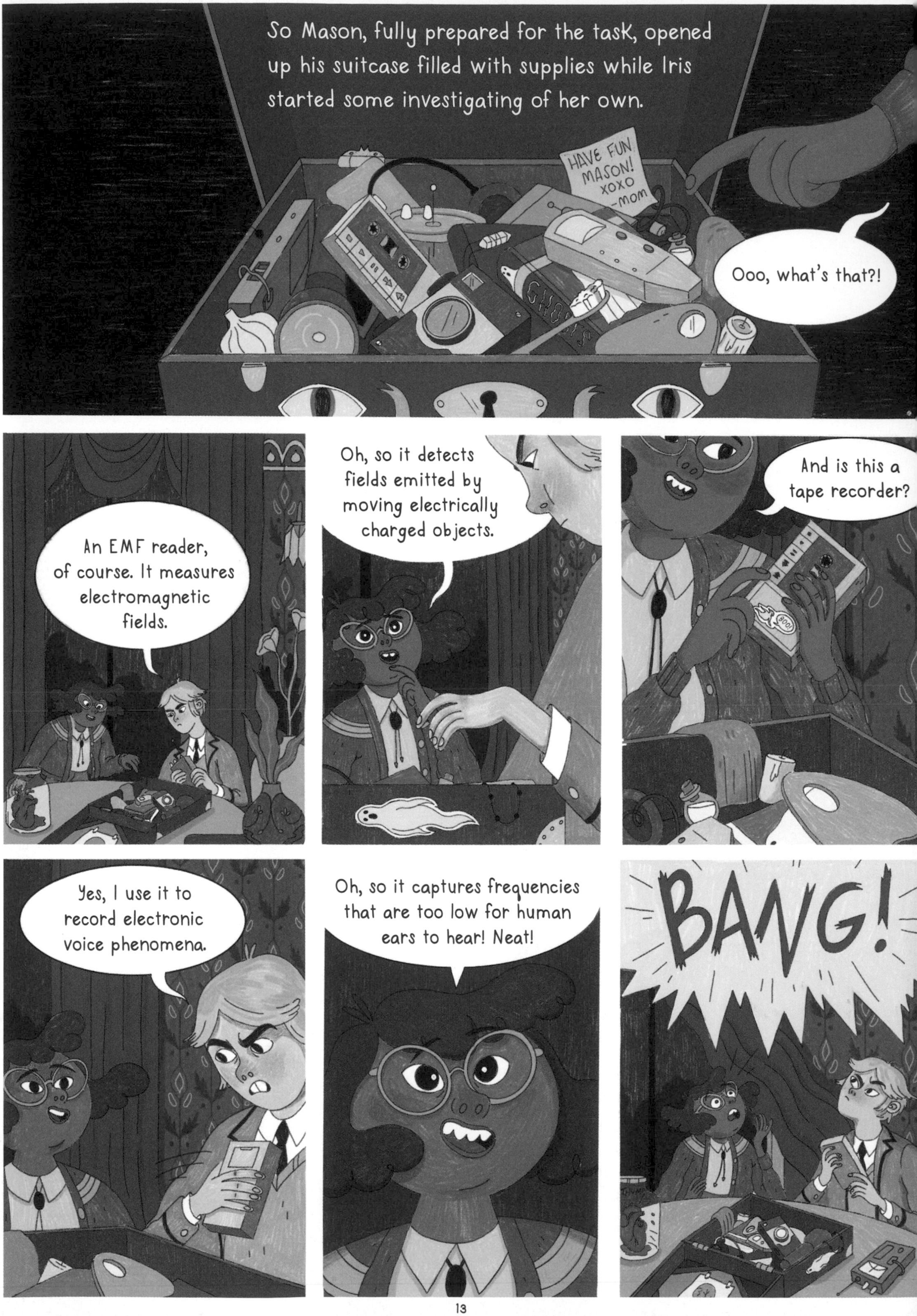

So Mason, fully prepared for the task, opened up his suitcase filled with supplies while Iris started some investigating of her own.
HAVE FUN, MASON! XOXO -MOM
Ooo, what's that?!
An EMF reader, of course. It measures electromagnetic fields.
Oh, so it detects fields emitted by moving electrically charged objects.
And is this a tape recorder?
Yes, I use it to record electronic voice phenomena.
Oh, so it captures frequencies that are too low for human ears to hear! Neat!
BANG!

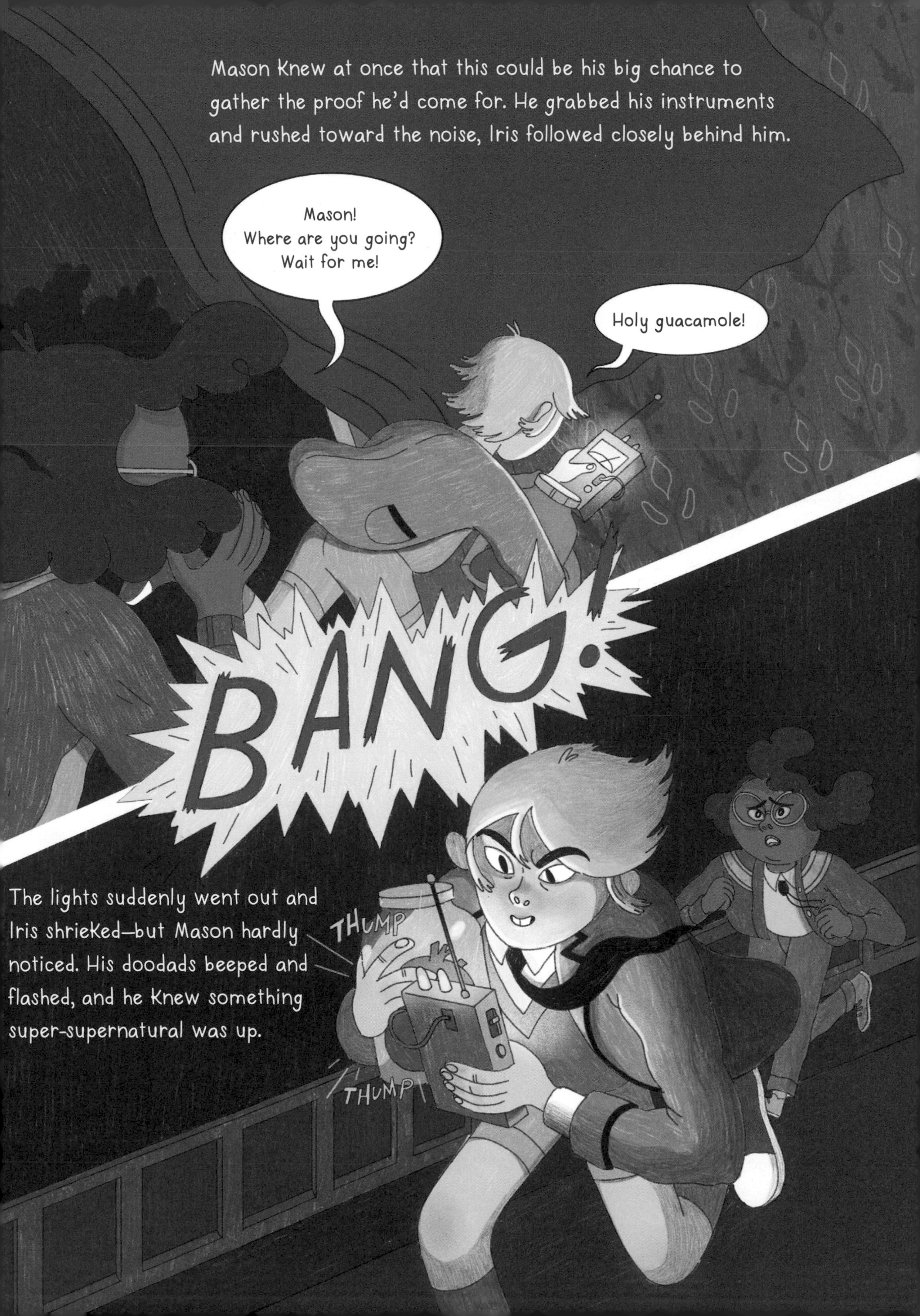
Mason knew at once that this could be his big chance to gather the proof he'd come for. He grabbed his instruments and rushed toward the noise, Iris followed closely behind him.
Mason! Where are you going? Wait for me!
Holy guacamole!
BANG!
The lights suddenly went out and Iris shrieked—but Mason hardly noticed. His doodads beeped and flashed, and he knew something super-supernatural was up.
THUMP
THUMP

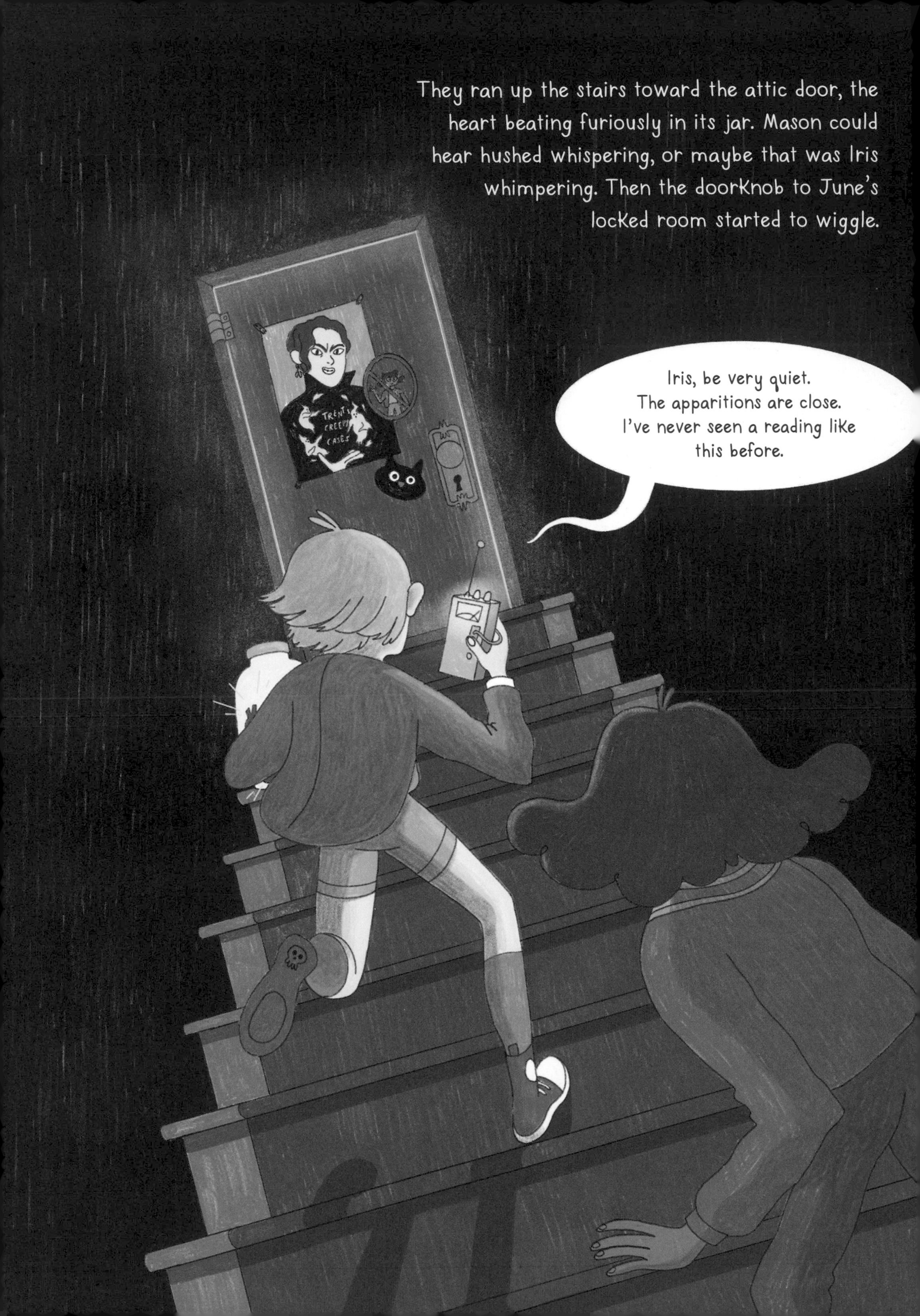
They ran up the stairs toward the attic door, the heart beating furiously in its jar. Mason could hear hushed whispering, or maybe that was Iris whimpering. Then the doorknob to June's locked room started to wiggle.
TRENT'S CREEPY CASES
Iris, be very quiet. The apparitions are close. I've never seen a reading like this before.

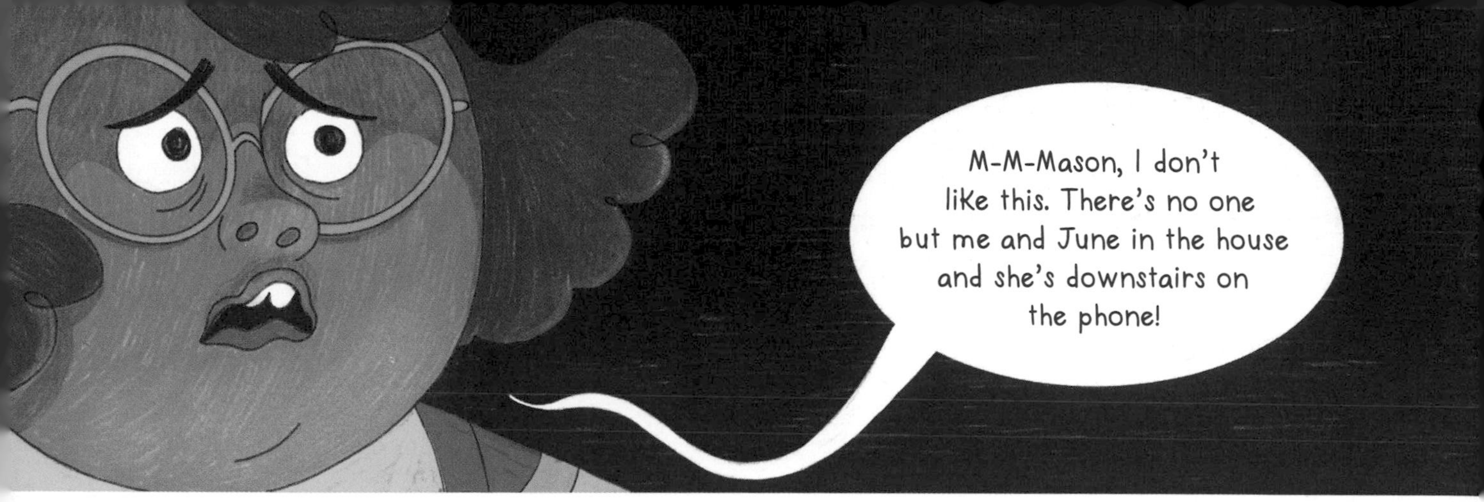
M-M-Mason, I don't like this. There's no one but me and June in the house and she's downstairs on the phone!

They heard the sound of the lock unclick and June's door handle turned slowly. Mason didn't hesitate for a second. Camera in hand, he knew this was it. This photo would make him famous. The door began to open. . . .

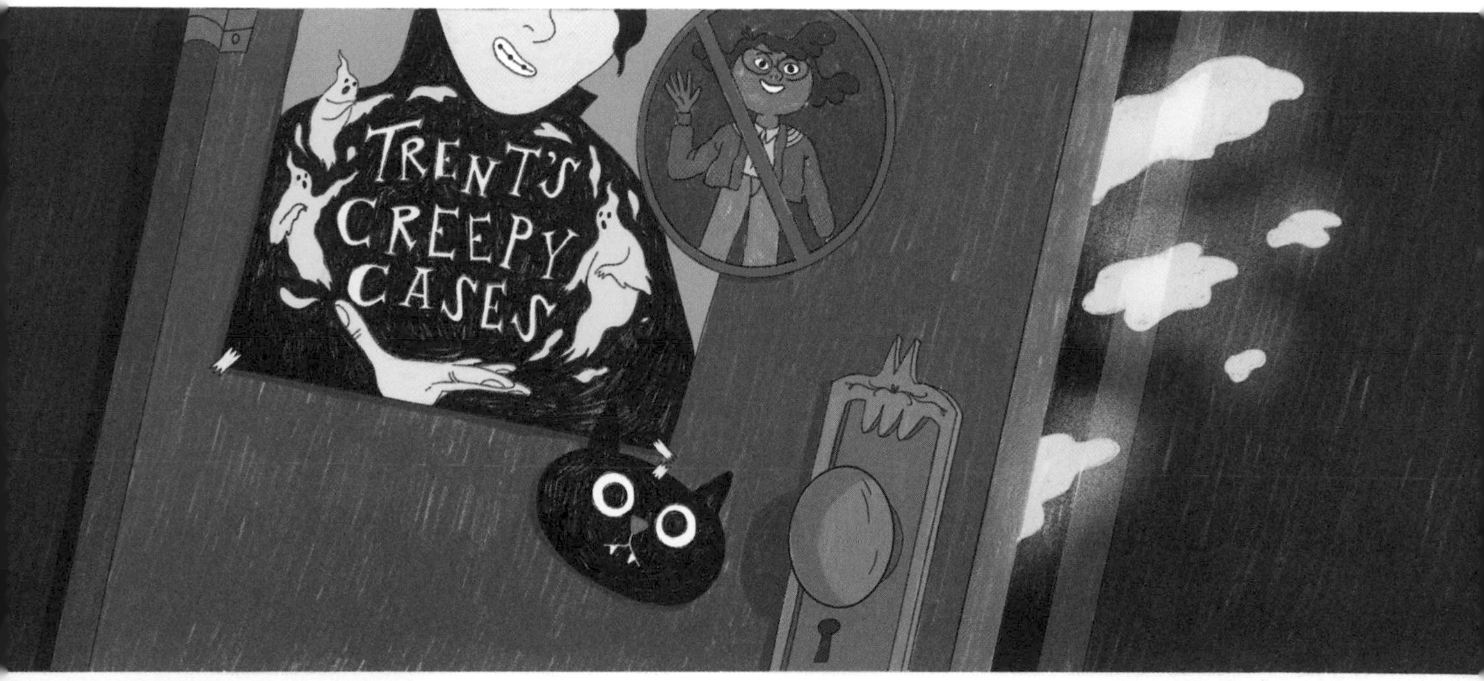
TRENT'S CREEPY CASES

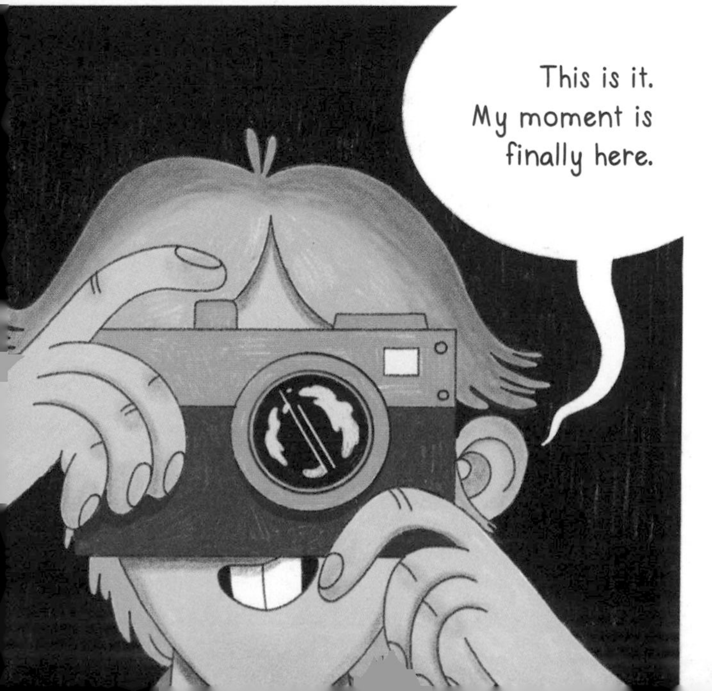
This is it. My moment is finally here.

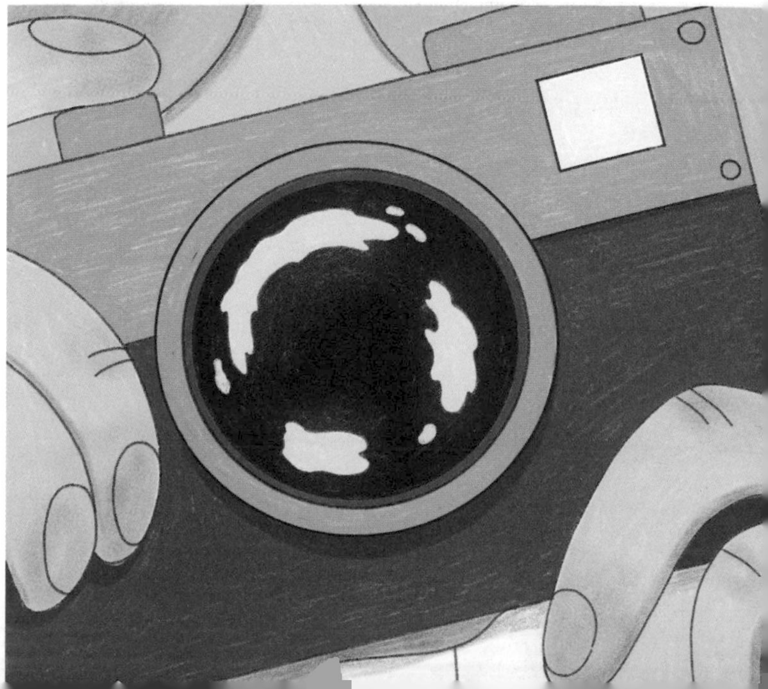

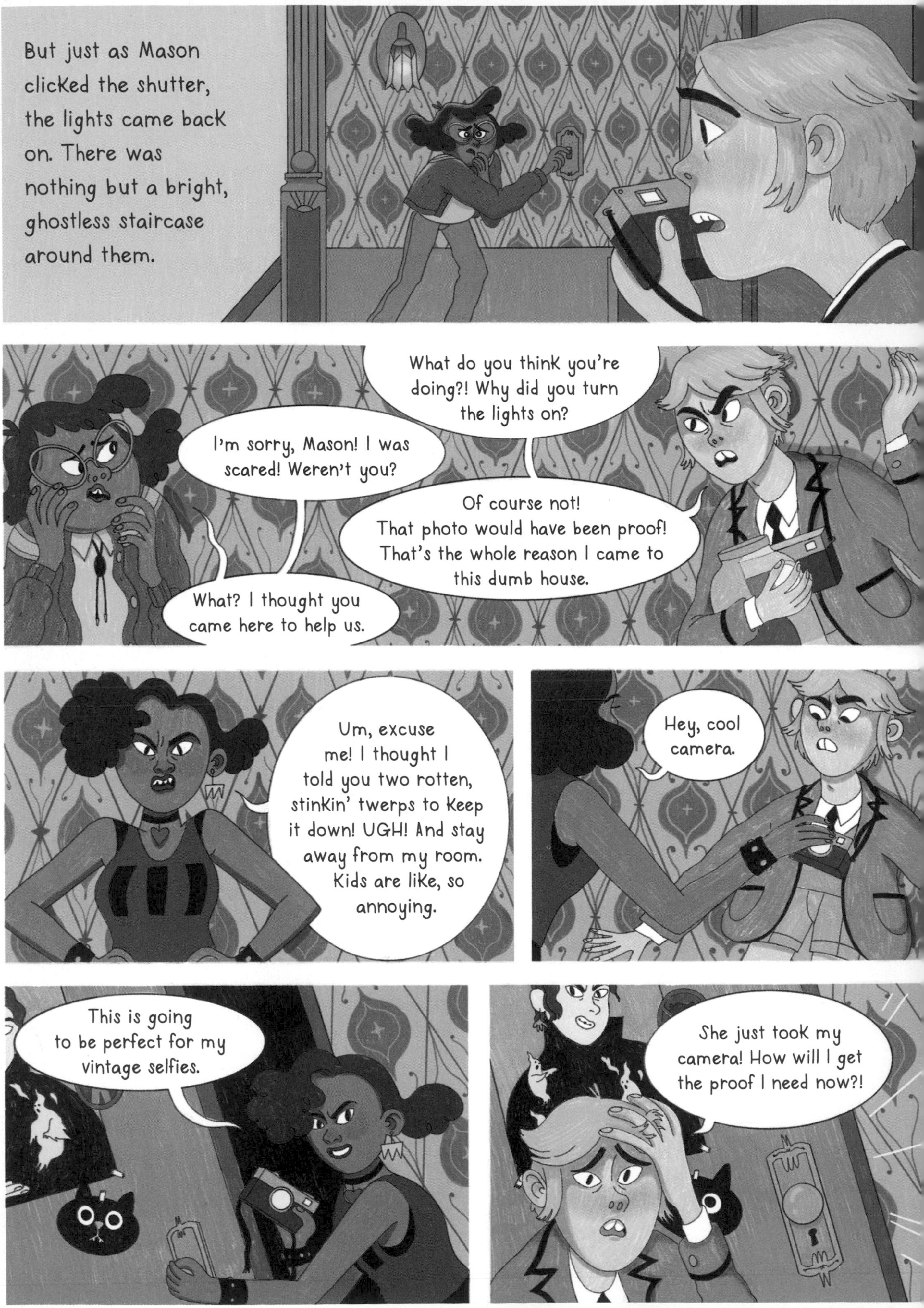
But just as Mason clicked the shutter, the lights came back on. There was nothing but a bright, ghostless staircase around them.
What do you think you're doing?! Why did you turn the lights on?
I'm sorry, Mason! I was scared! Weren't you?
Of course not! That photo would have been proof! That's the whole reason I came to this dumb house.
What? I thought you came here to help us.
Um, excuse me! I thought I told you two rotten, stinkin' twerps to keep it down! UGH! And stay away from my room. Kids are like, so annoying.
Hey, cool camera.
This is going to be perfect for my vintage selfies.
She just took my camera! How will I get the proof I need now?!

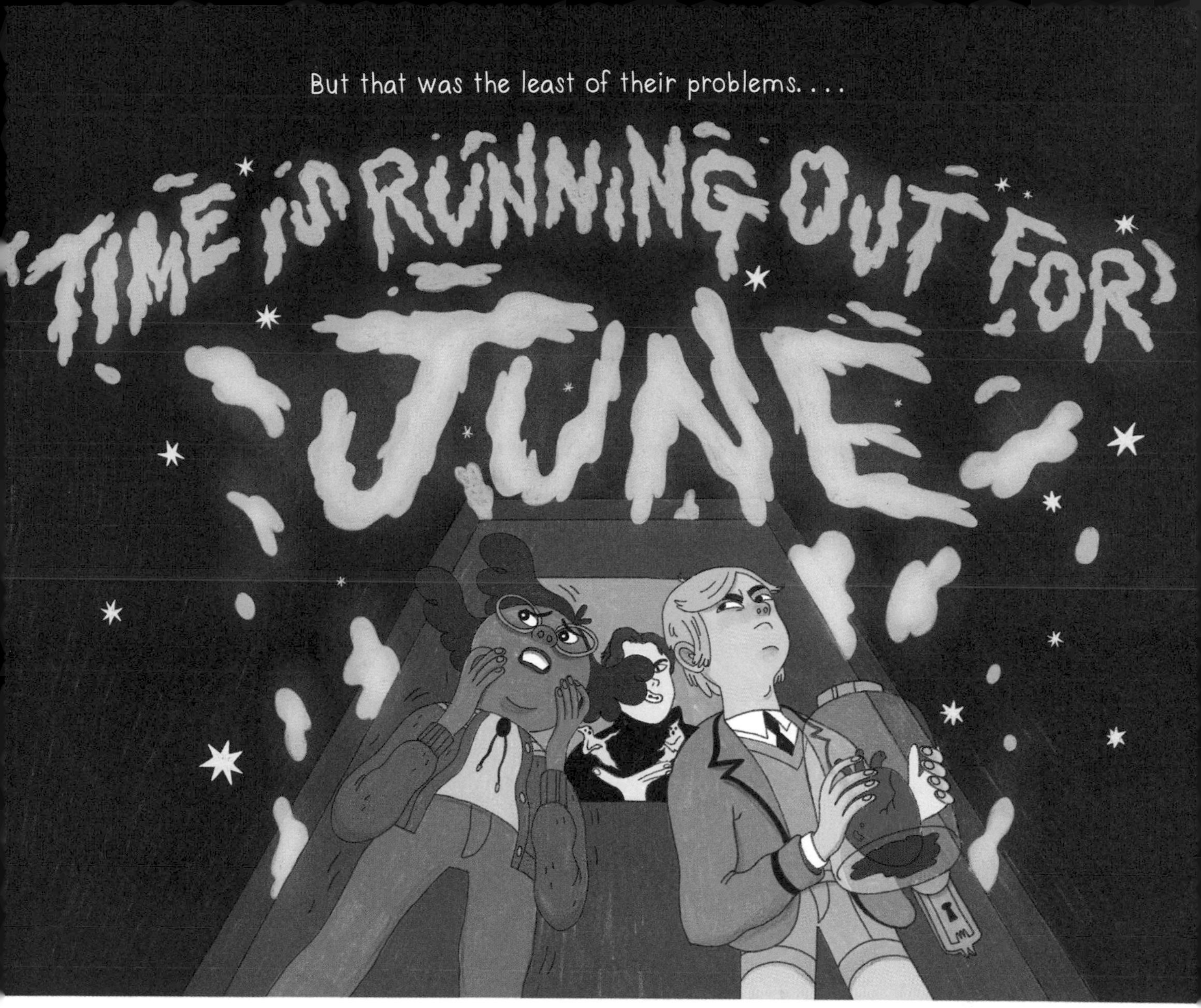
But that was the least of their problems. . . .
TIME IS RUNNING OUT FOR JUNE

With that, Mason knew what he had to do. It was time to leave the realm of cold, hard facts and all that nonsense behind, and enter the world of the mysterious.

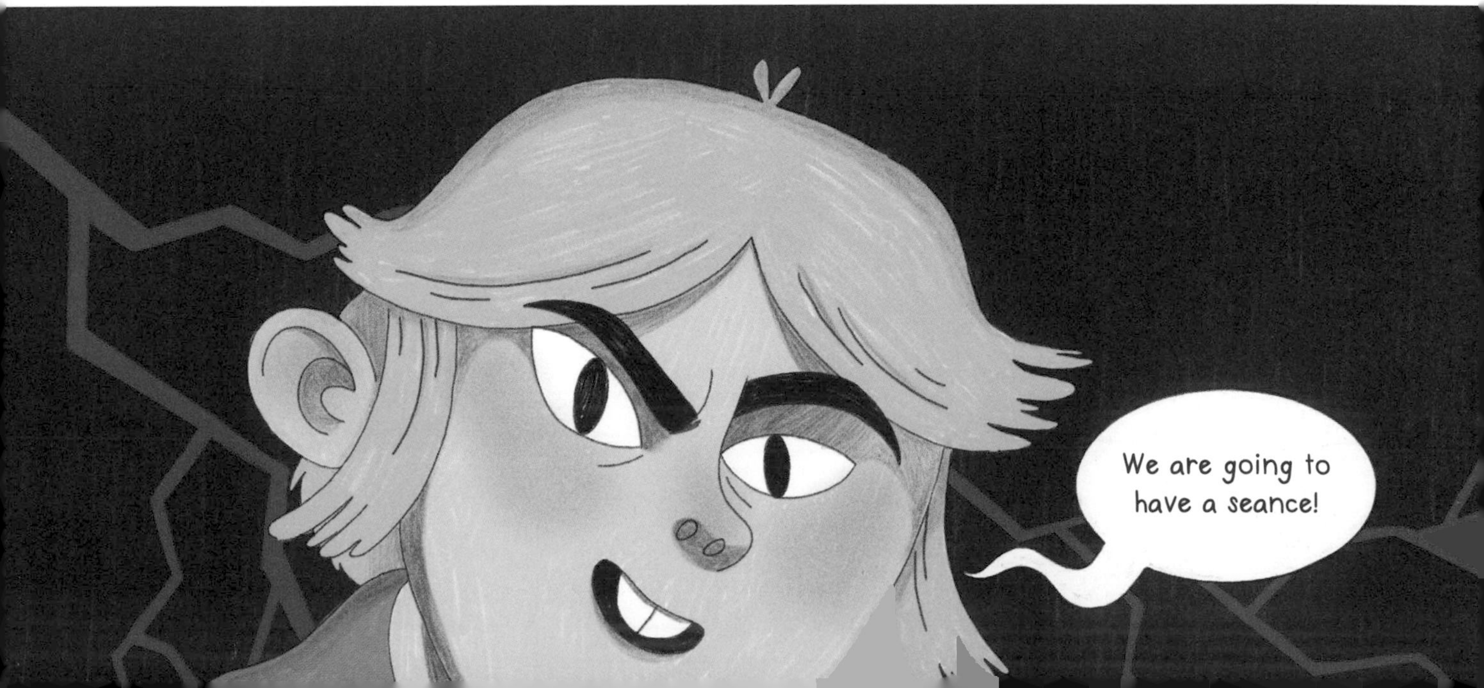
We are going to have a seance!

The thing about seances is that they are mostly a bunch of baloney. A lot of hooey, if you will. But occasionally something strange happens. . . . Mason was counting on this being one of those times. He lit some vanilla candles—because if you're going to dabble in the world of the supernatural, you want it to smell nice—then he and a very nervous Iris sat down and prepared themselves.

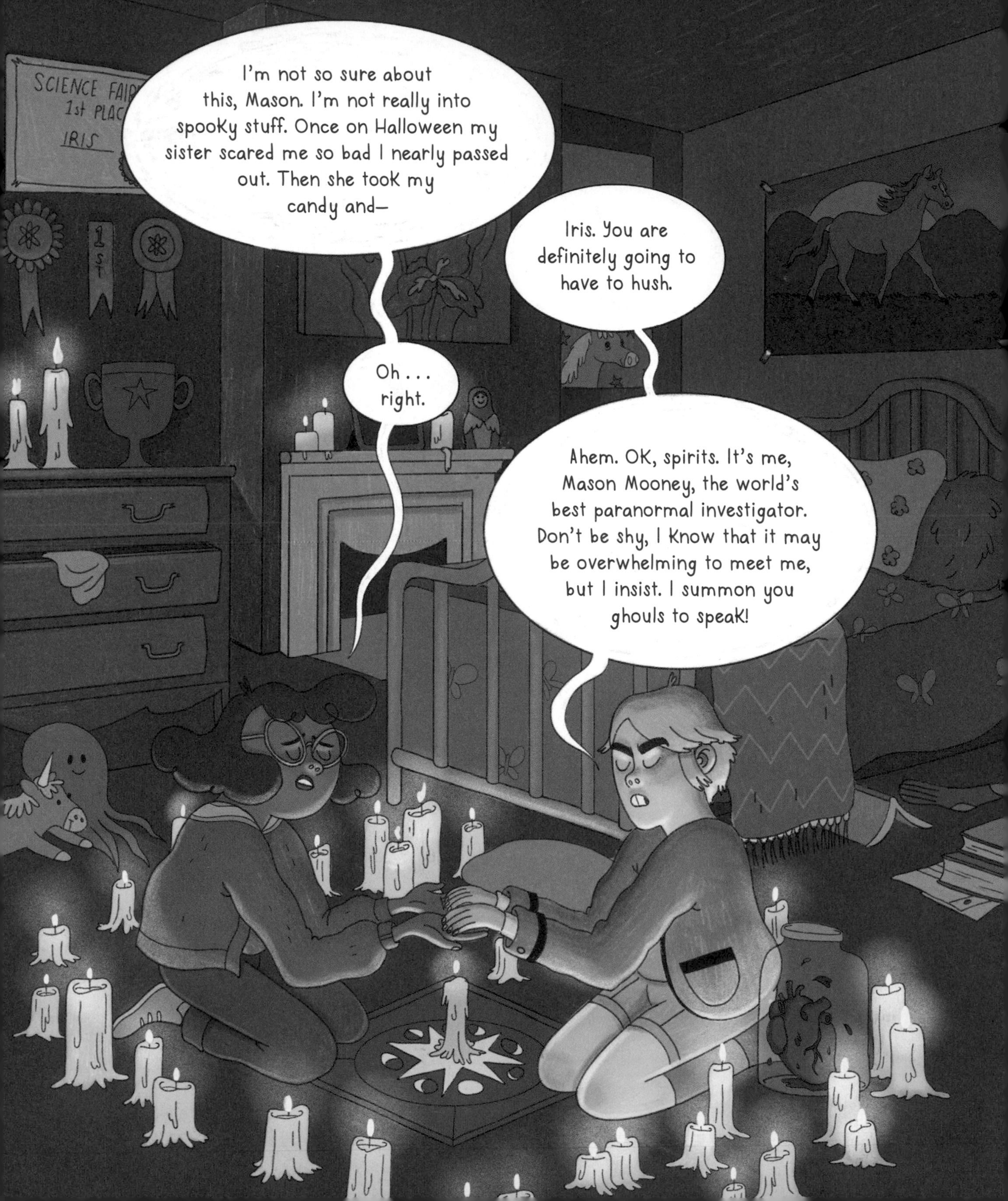
I'm not so sure about this, Mason. I'm not really into spooky stuff. Once on Halloween my sister scared me so bad I nearly passed out. Then she took my candy and—
Iris. You are definitely going to have to hush.
Oh . . . right.
Ahem. OK, spirits. It's me, Mason Mooney, the world's best paranormal investigator. Don't be shy, I know that it may be overwhelming to meet me, but I insist. I summon you ghouls to speak!

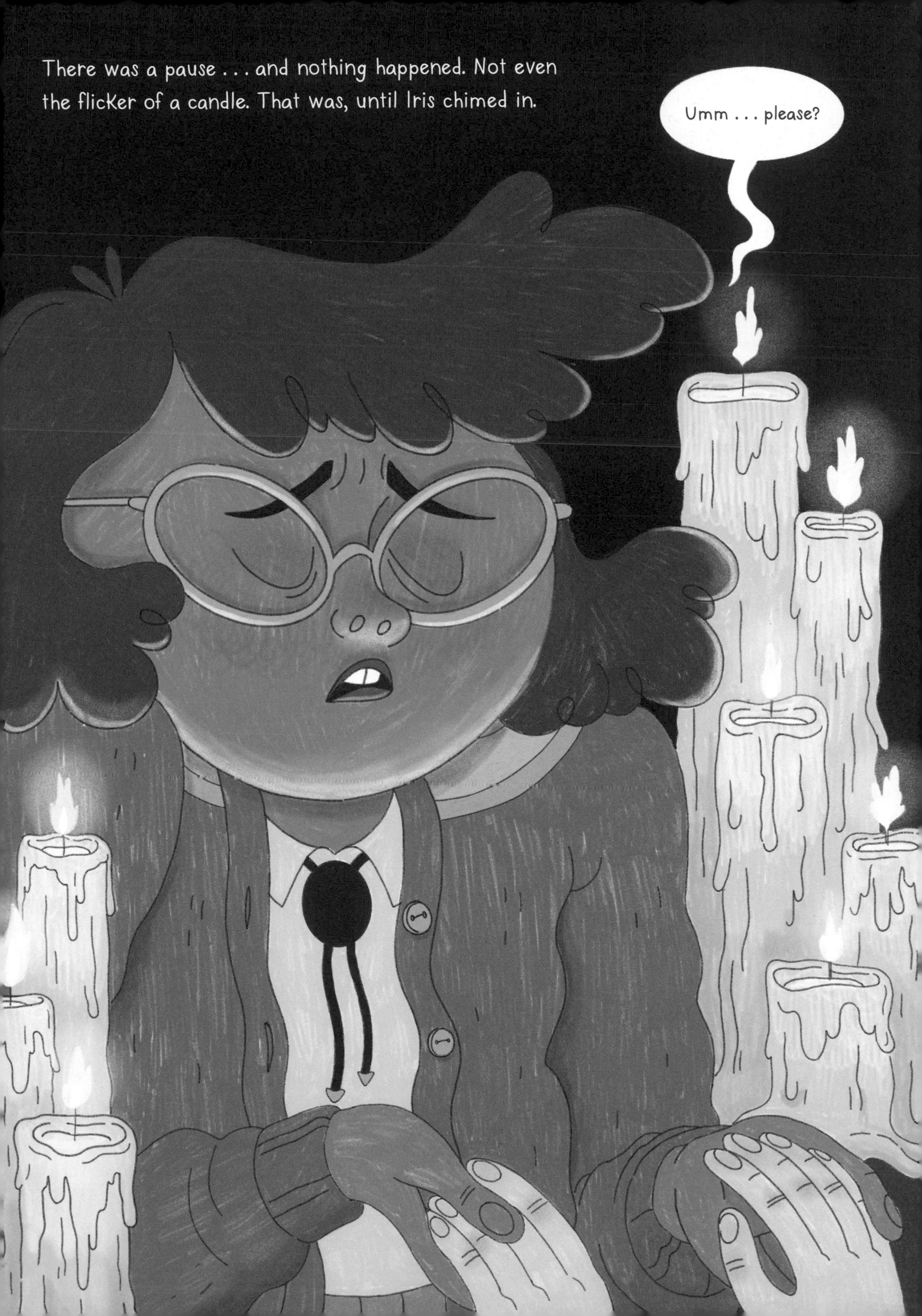
There was a pause . . . and nothing happened. Not even the flicker of a candle. That was, until Iris chimed in.
Umm . . . please?

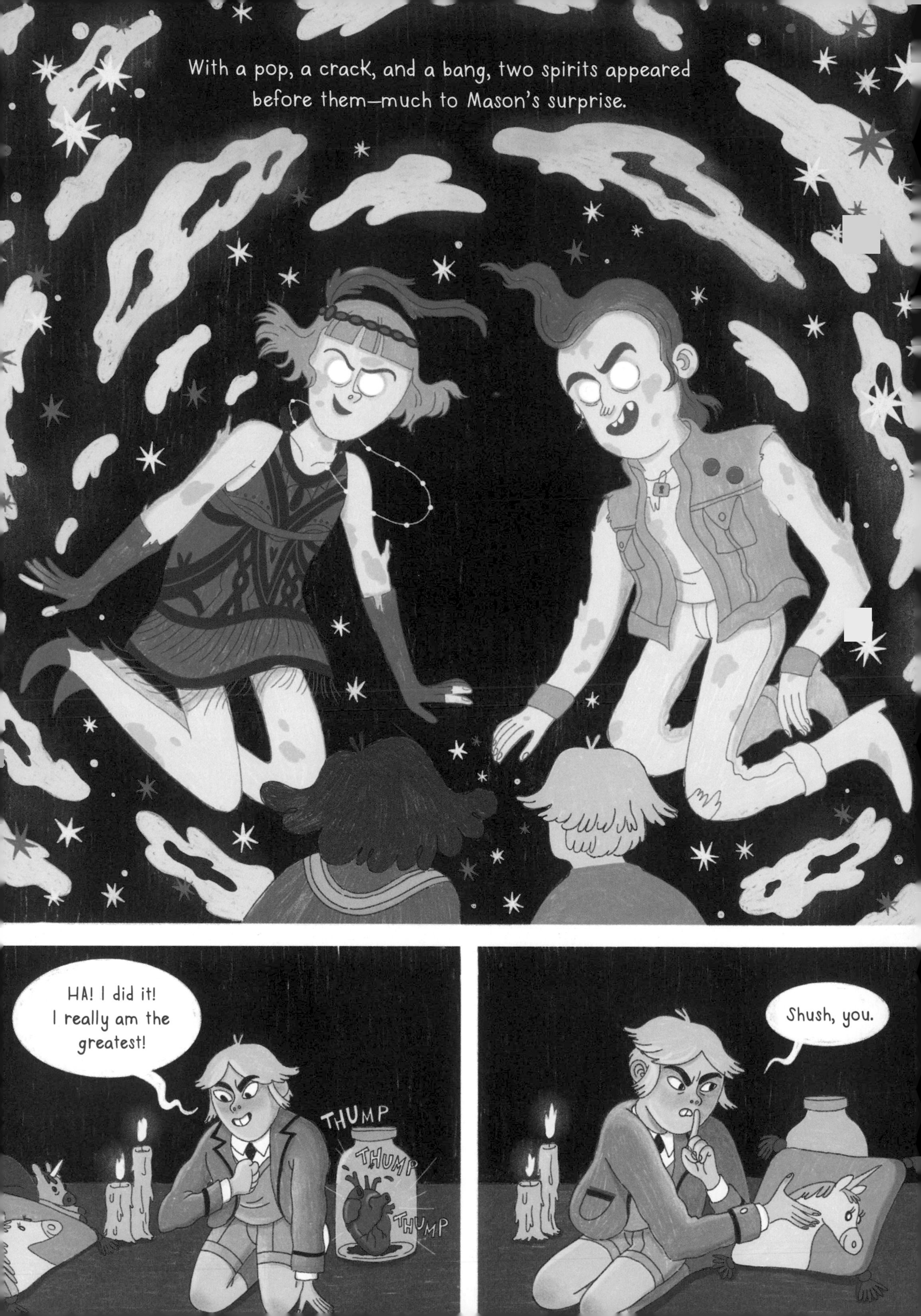
With a pop, a crack, and a bang, two spirits appeared before them—much to Mason's surprise.
HA! I did it! I really am the greatest!
THUMP
THUMP
THUMP
Shush, you.

This boy thinks a lot of himself, doesn't he? I mean, who is he? I've never heard of him.

Totally! It's quite off-putting. Maybe he's friends with that investigator June is obsessed with?

Say young man, do you know that dreamboat, Trent Reilly? The one who's on the funny box with moving pictures?

Oh, for the last time. It's a TELEVISION!

How am I supposed to remember that? In my day, we had no need for such tedious forms of entertainment. We had parties to attend, where we could shake our tushies all night long.

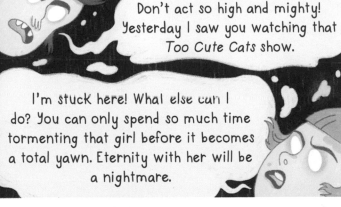

Don't act so high and mighty! Yesterday I saw you watching that *Too Cute Cats* show.

I'm stuck here! What else can I do? You can only spend so much time tormenting that girl before it becomes a total yawn. Eternity with her will be a nightmare.

What do you mean eternity?!

Suddenly the room began to grow noticeably colder. Every single hair on the back of Iris' neck stood on end and her teeth began to chatter.

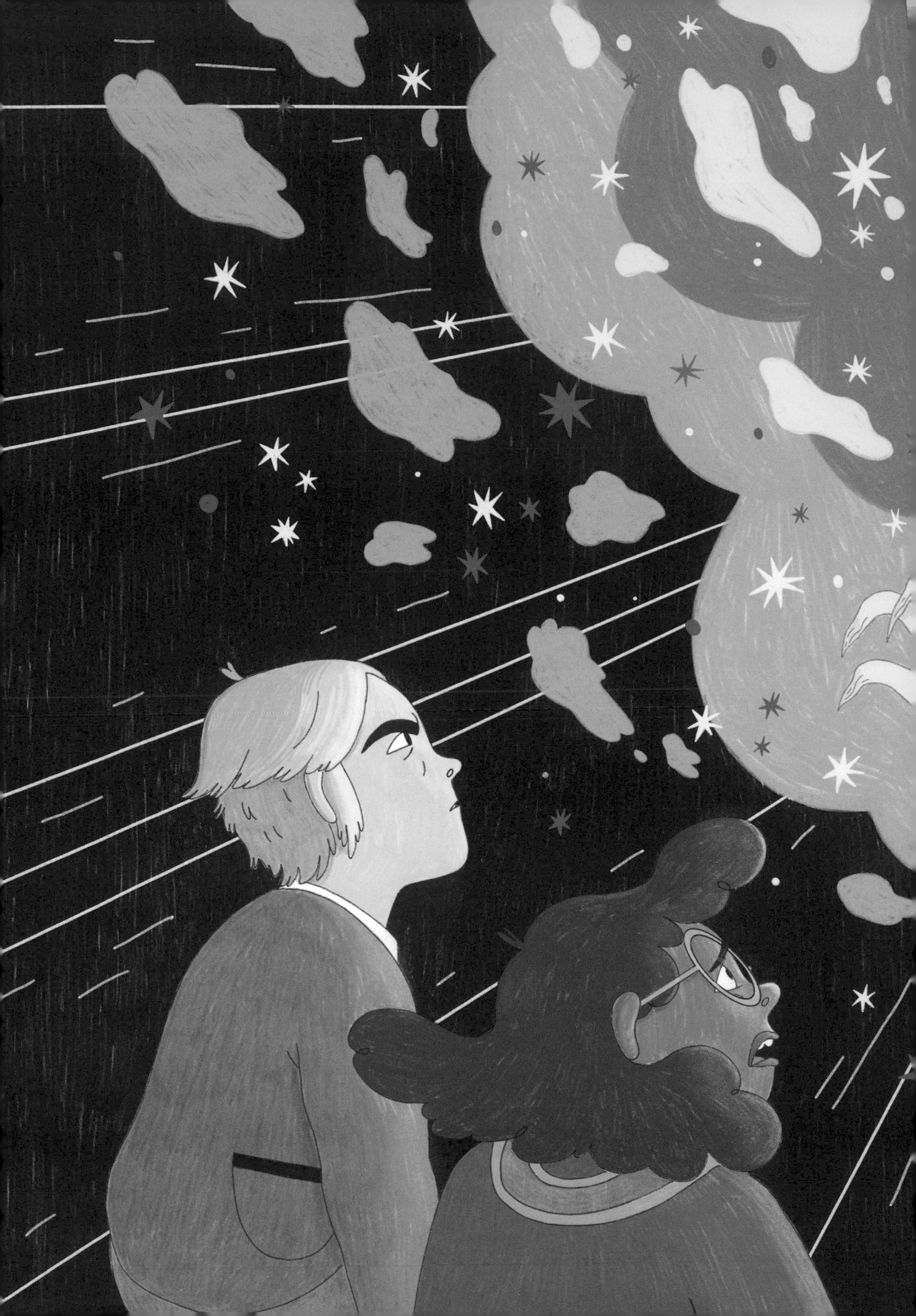

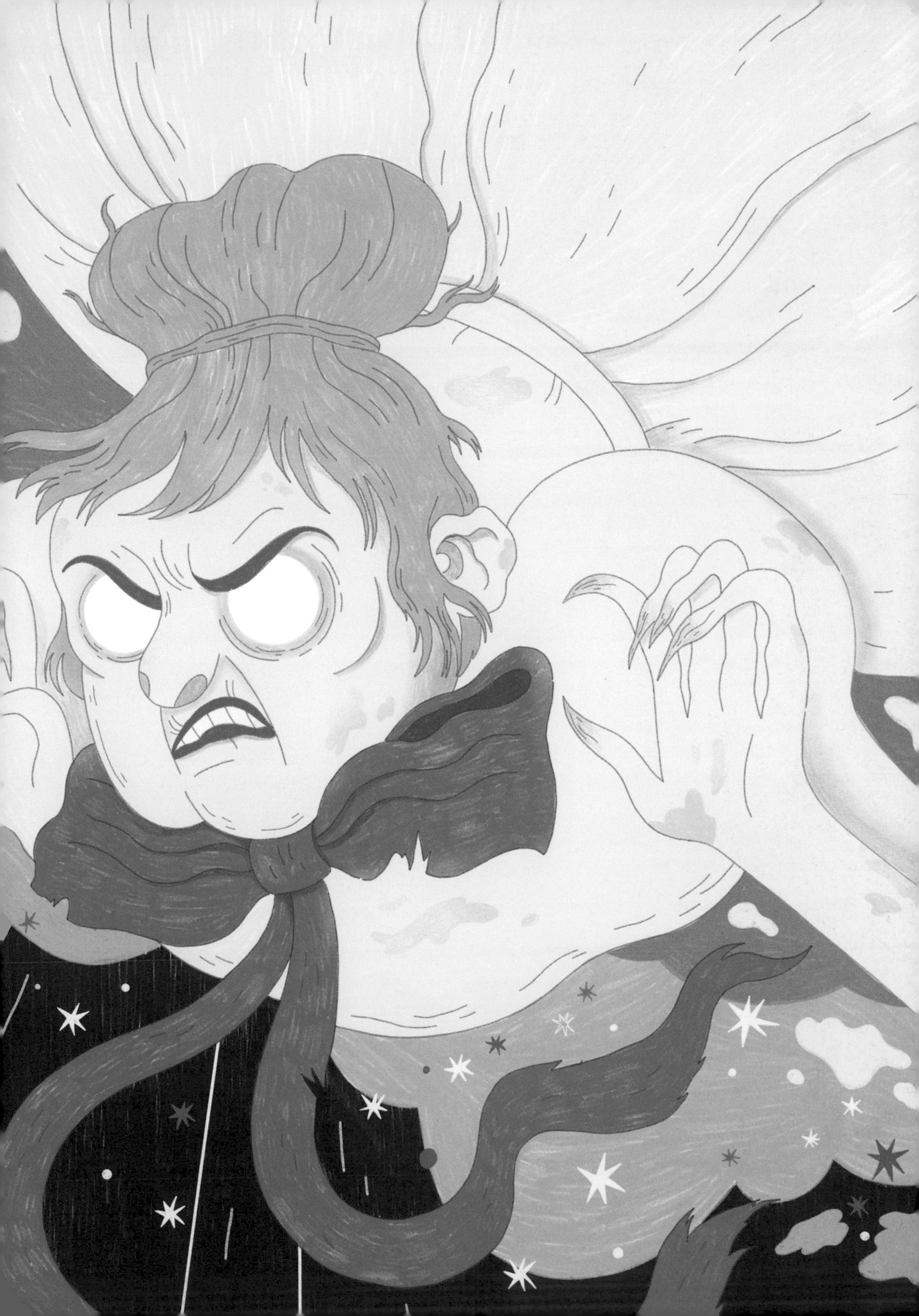

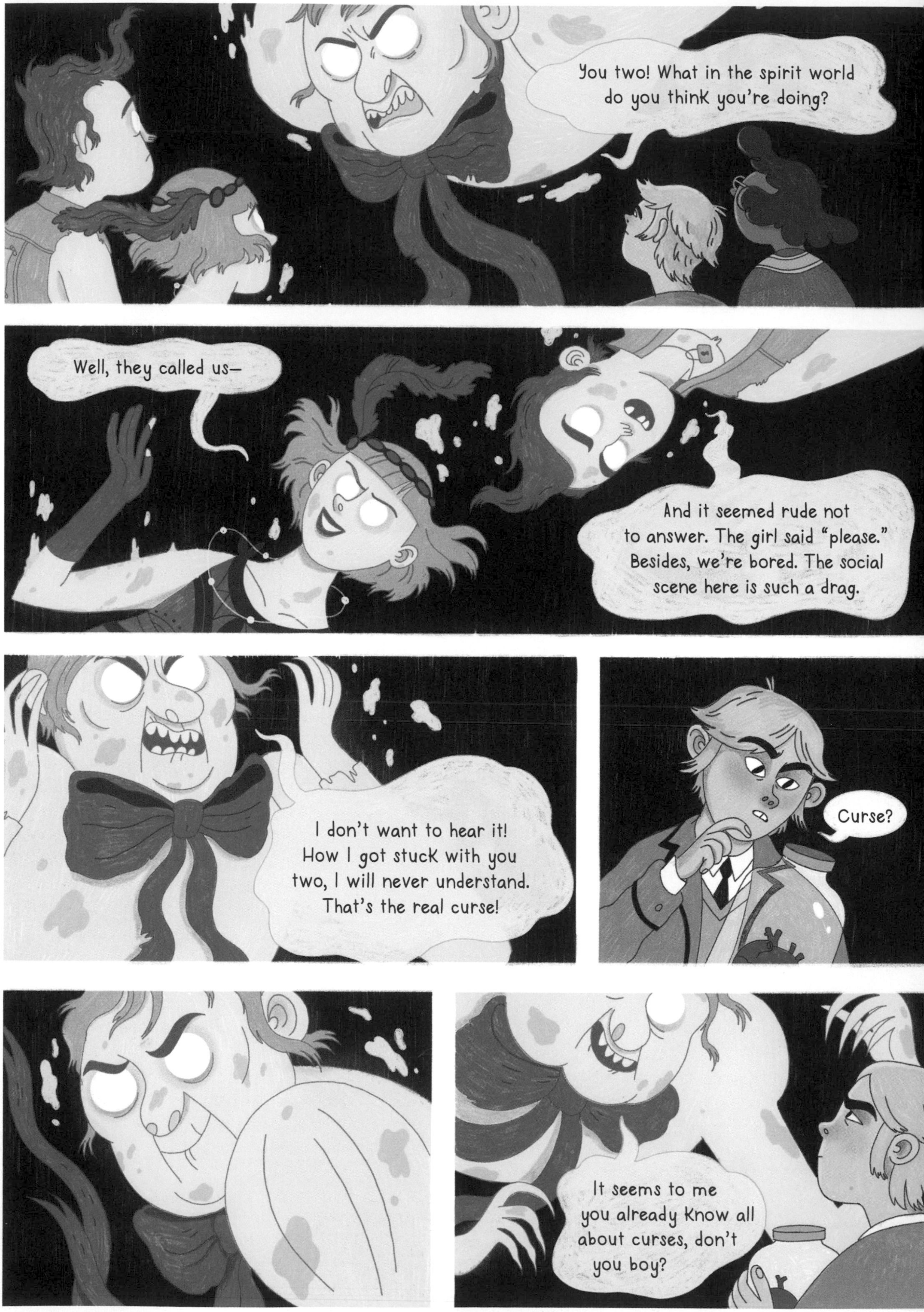
You two! What in the spirit world do you think you're doing?
Well, they called us—
And it seemed rude not to answer. The girl said "please." Besides, we're bored. The social scene here is such a drag.
I don't want to hear it! How I got stuck with you two, I will never understand. That's the real curse!
Curse?
It seems to me you already know all about curses, don't you boy?

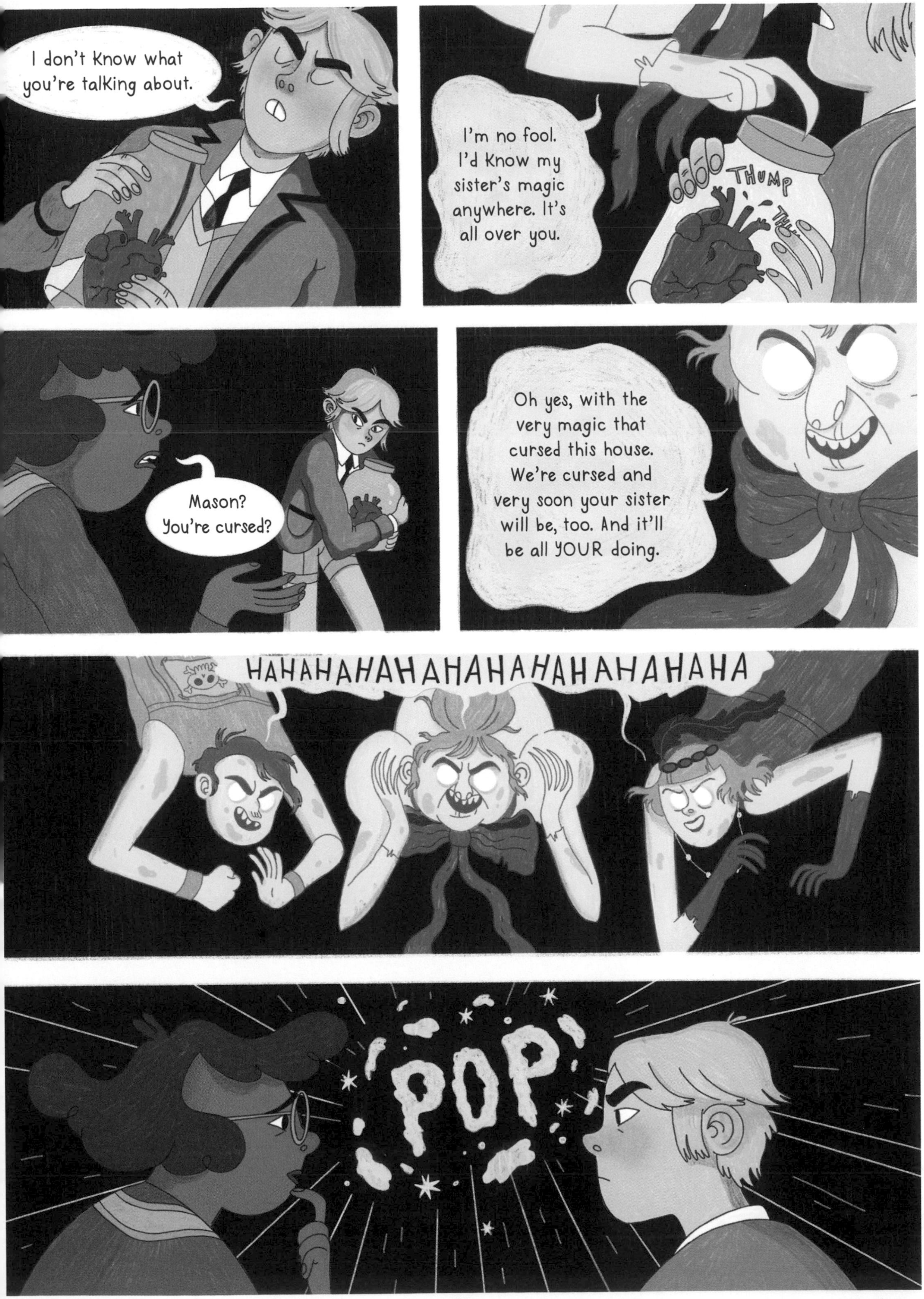
I don't know what you're talking about.
I'm no fool. I'd know my sister's magic anywhere. It's all over you.
THUMP
THU...
Mason? You're cursed?
Oh yes, with the very magic that cursed this house. We're cursed and very soon your sister will be, too. And it'll be all YOUR doing.
HAHAHAHAHAHAHAHAHAHAHAHAHA
POP

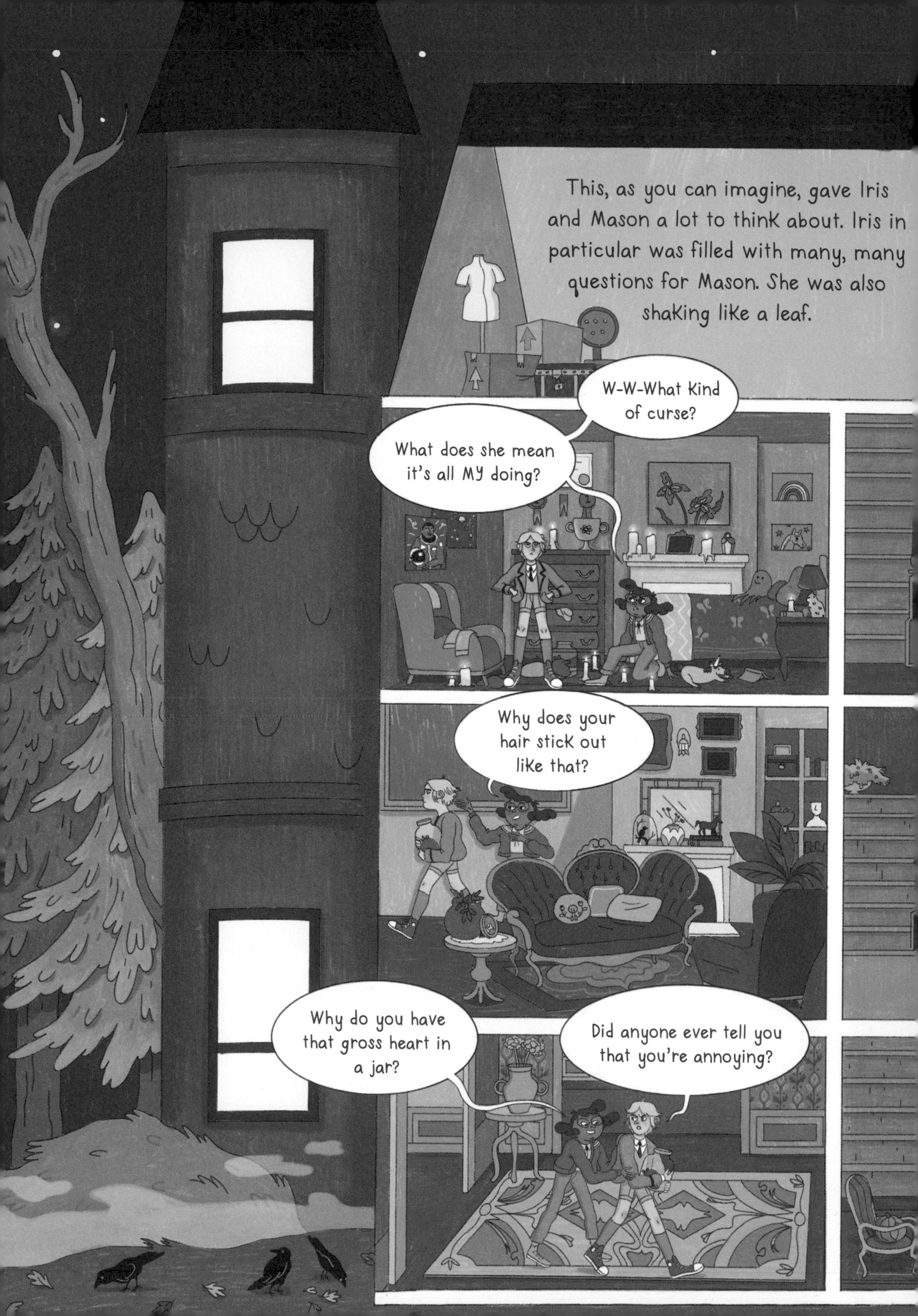

This, as you can imagine, gave Iris and Mason a lot to think about. Iris in particular was filled with many, many questions for Mason. She was also shaking like a leaf.
W-W-What Kind of curse?
What does she mean it's all MY doing?
Why does your hair stick out like that?
Why do you have that gross heart in a jar?
Did anyone ever tell you that you're annoying?

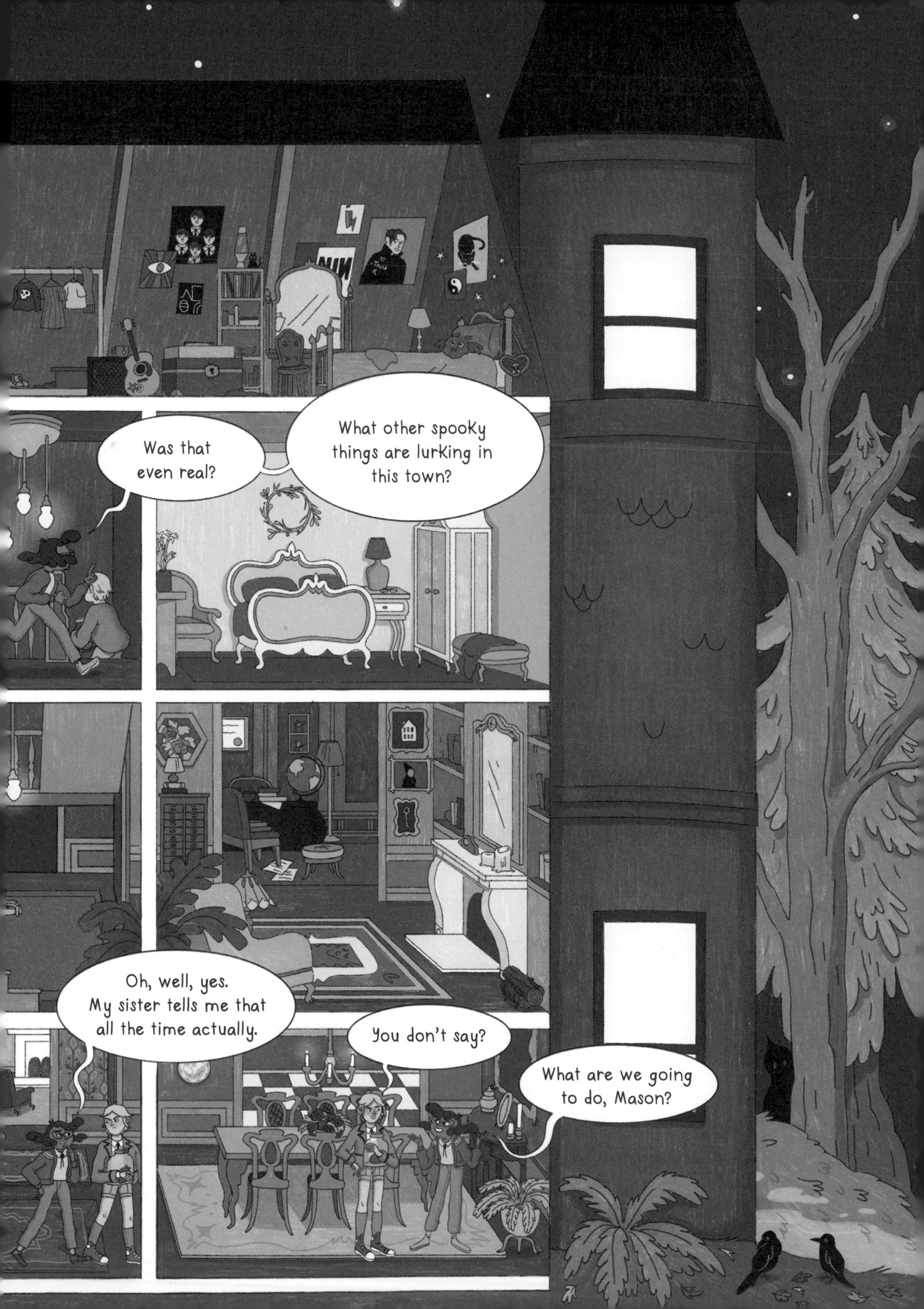
Was that even real?
What other spooky things are lurking in this town?
Oh, well, yes. My sister tells me that all the time actually.
You don't say?
What are we going to do, Mason?

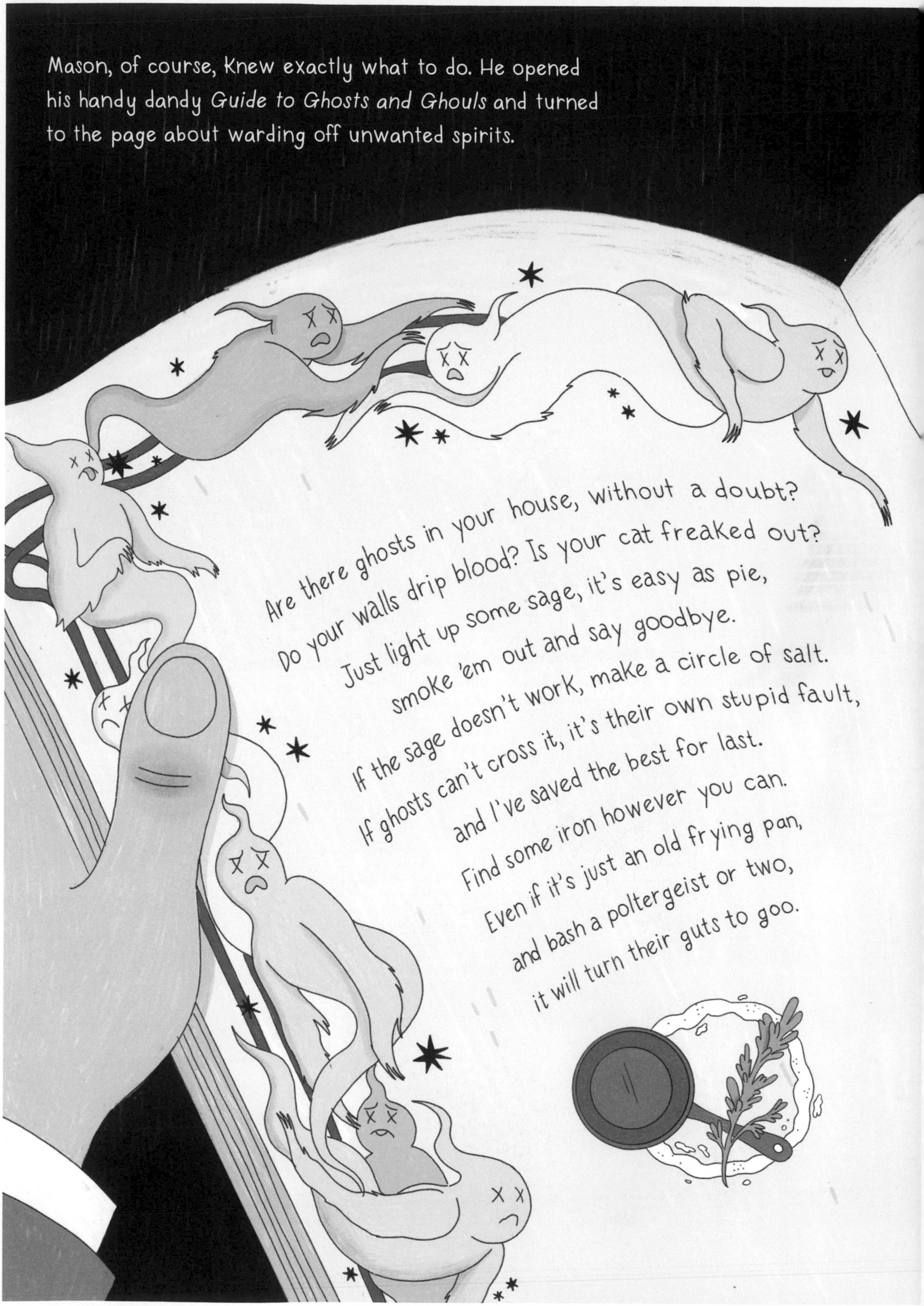
Mason, of course, knew exactly what to do. He opened his handy dandy *Guide to Ghosts and Ghouls* and turned to the page about warding off unwanted spirits.
Are there ghosts in your house, without a doubt?
Do your walls drip blood? Is your cat freaked out?
Just light up some sage, it's easy as pie,
smoke 'em out and say goodbye.
If the sage doesn't work, make a circle of salt.
If ghosts can't cross it, it's their own stupid fault,
and I've saved the best for last.
Find some iron however you can.
Even if it's just an old frying pan,
and bash a poltergeist or two,
it will turn their guts to goo.

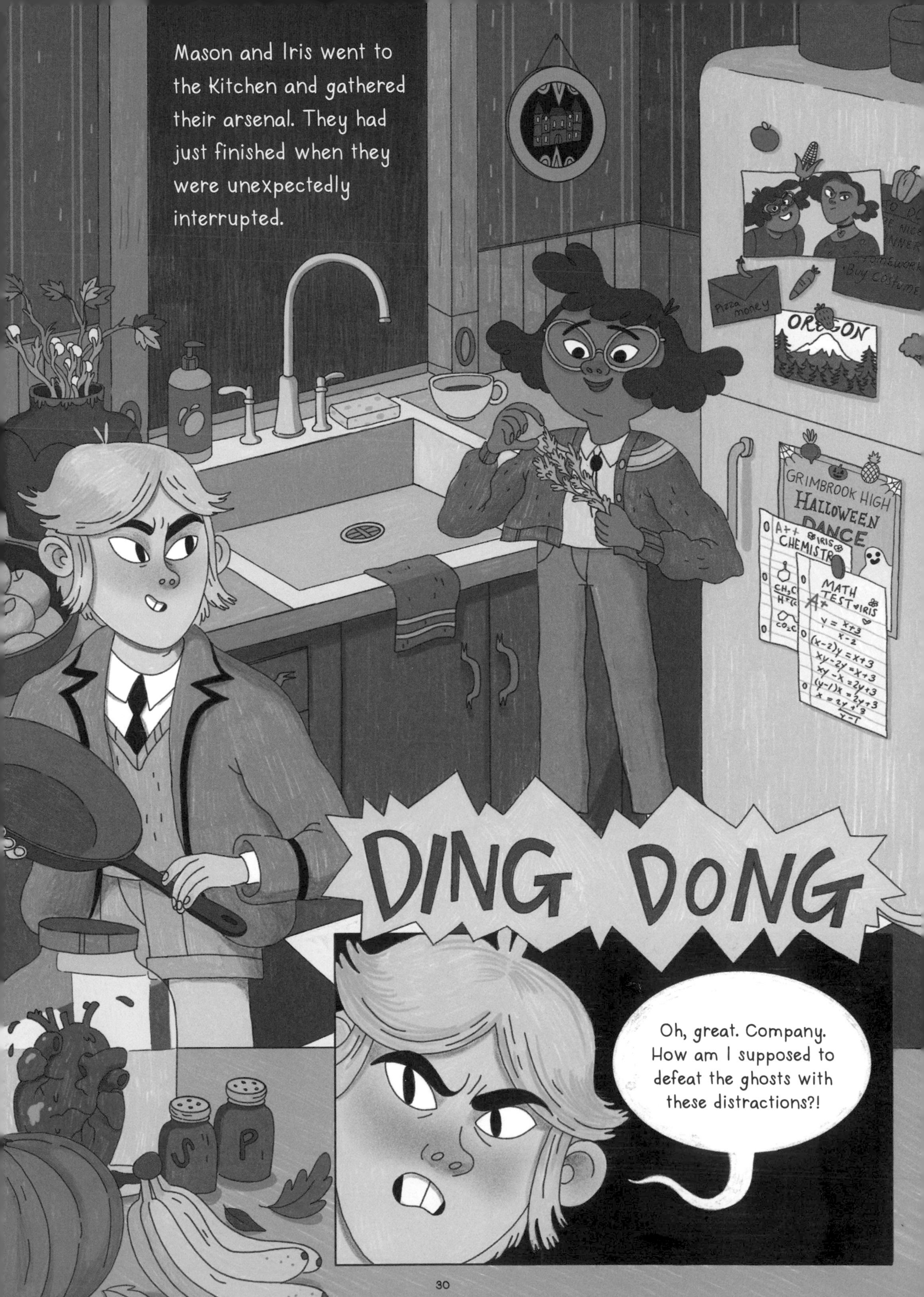
Mason and Iris went to the Kitchen and gathered their arsenal. They had just finished when they were unexpectedly interrupted.
OREGON
GRIMBROOK HIGH HALLOWEEN DANCE
DING DONG
Oh, great. Company. How am I supposed to defeat the ghosts with these distractions?!

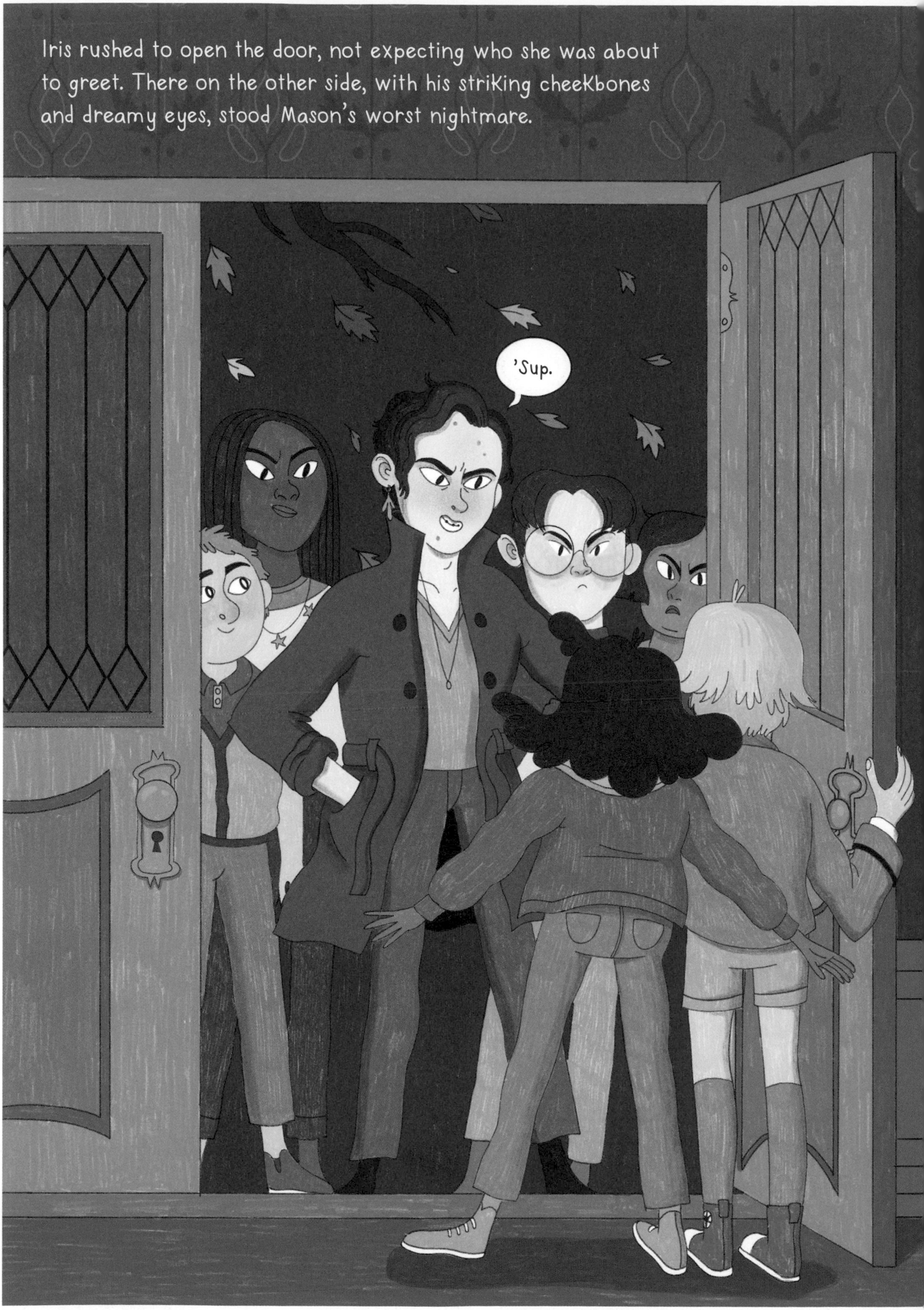
Iris rushed to open the door, not expecting who she was about to greet. There on the other side, with his striking cheekbones and dreamy eyes, stood Mason's worst nightmare.
'Sup.

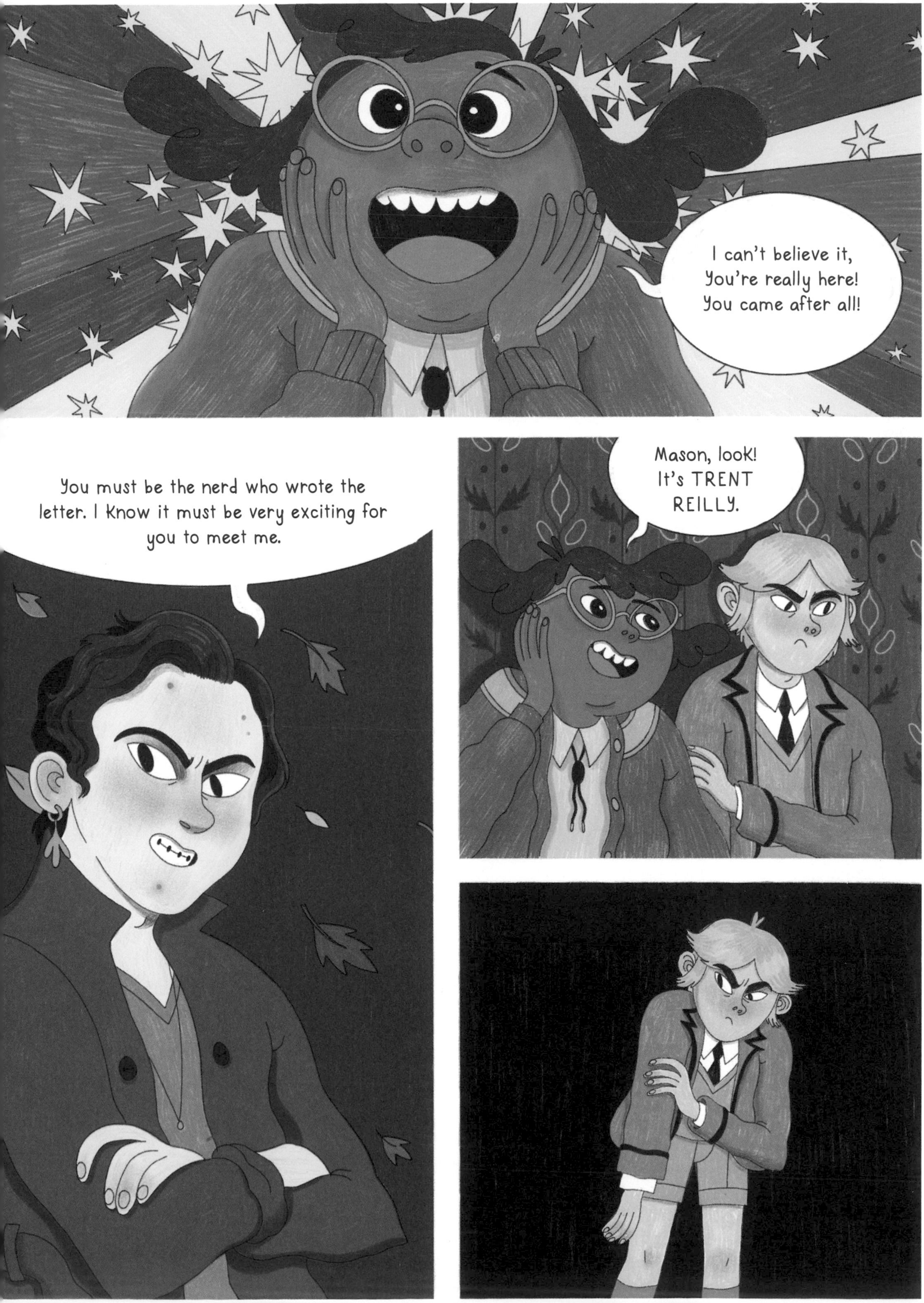
I can't believe it, You're really here! You came after all!
You must be the nerd who wrote the letter. I know it must be very exciting for you to meet me.
Mason, look! It's TRENT REILLY.

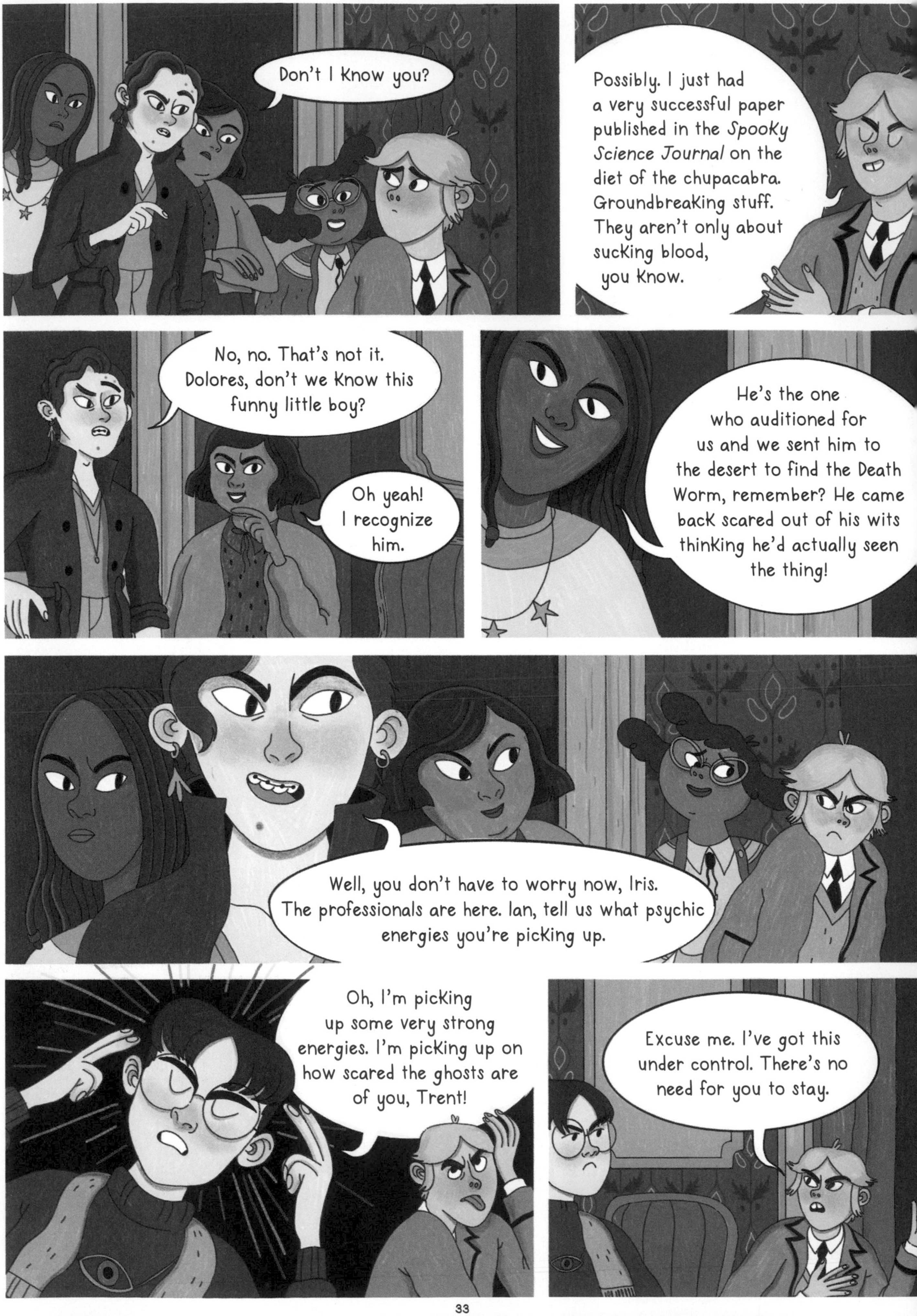
Don't I Know you?
Possibly. I just had a very successful paper published in the *Spooky Science Journal* on the diet of the chupacabra. Groundbreaking stuff. They aren't only about sucking blood, you Know.
No, no. That's not it. Dolores, don't we Know this funny little boy?
Oh yeah! I recognize him.
He's the one who auditioned for us and we sent him to the desert to find the Death Worm, remember? He came back scared out of his wits thinking he'd actually seen the thing!
Well, you don't have to worry now, Iris. The professionals are here. Ian, tell us what psychic energies you're picking up.
Oh, I'm picking up some very strong energies. I'm picking up on how scared the ghosts are of you, Trent!
Excuse me. I've got this under control. There's no need for you to stay.

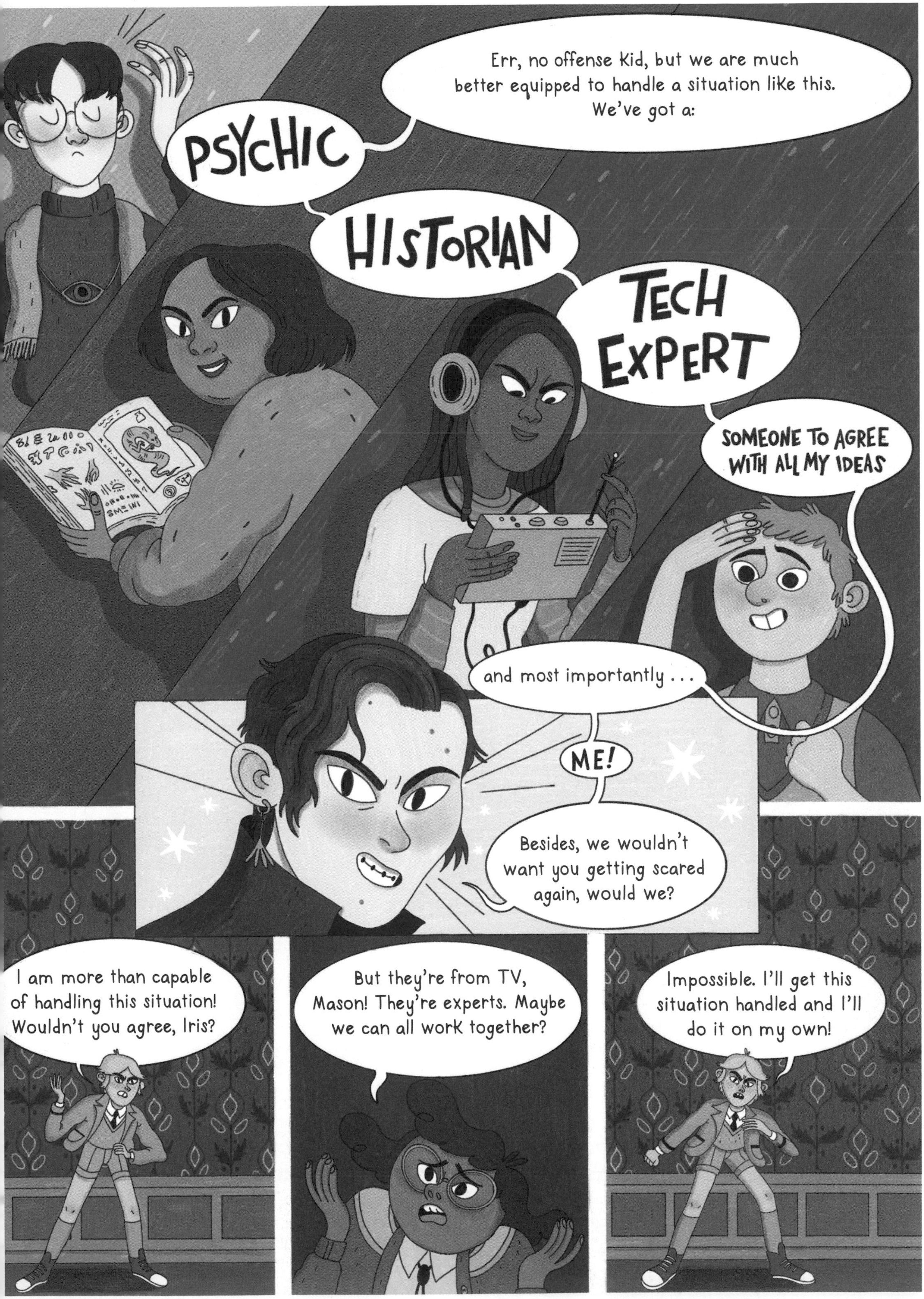
Err, no offense Kid, but we are much better equipped to handle a situation like this. We've got a:
PSYCHIC
HISTORIAN
TECH EXPERT
SOMEONE TO AGREE WITH ALL MY IDEAS
and most importantly . . .
ME!
Besides, we wouldn't want you getting scared again, would we?
I am more than capable of handling this situation! Wouldn't you agree, Iris?
But they're from TV, Mason! They're experts. Maybe we can all work together?
Impossible. I'll get this situation handled and I'll do it on my own!

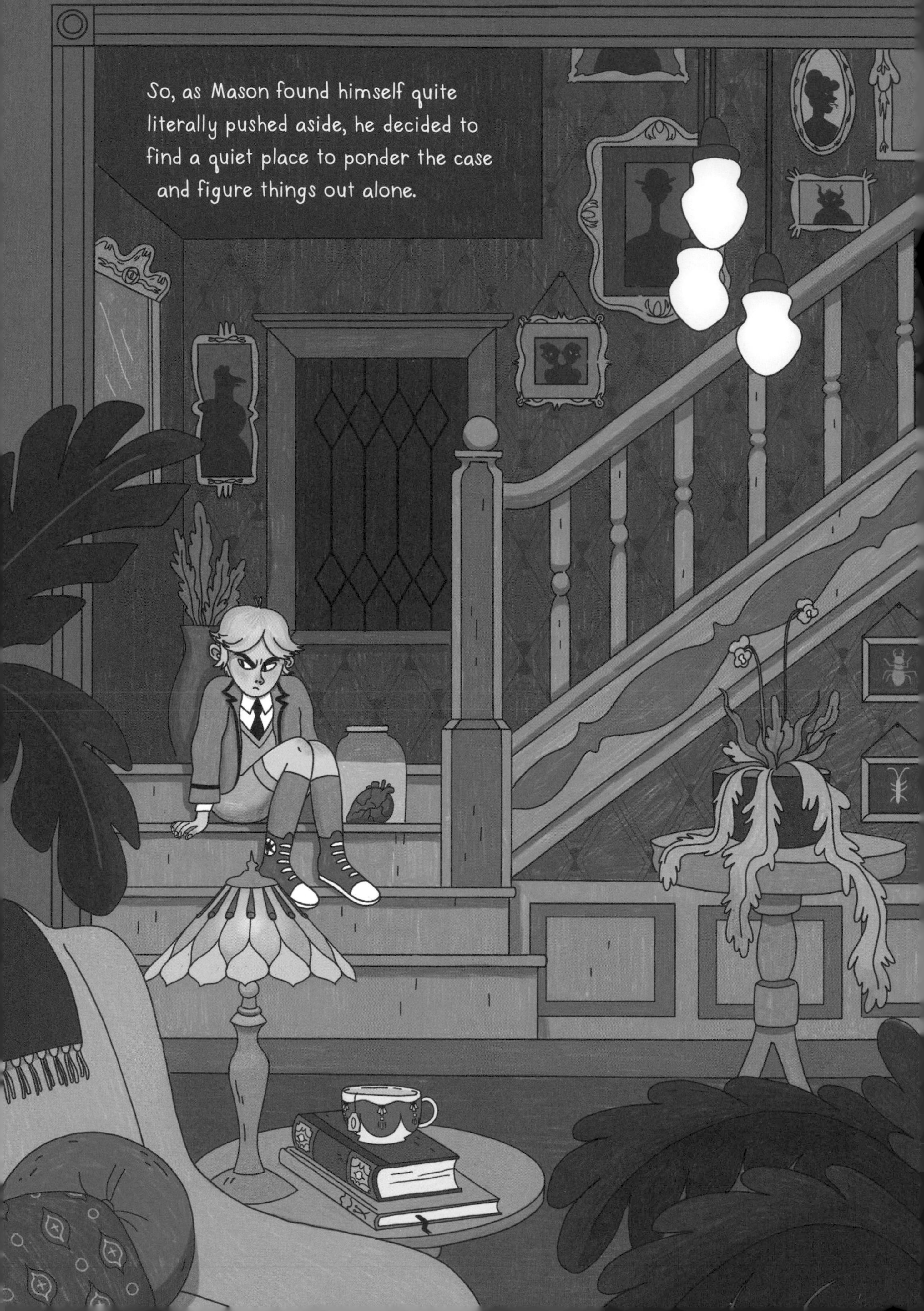
So, as Mason found himself quite literally pushed aside, he decided to find a quiet place to ponder the case and figure things out alone.

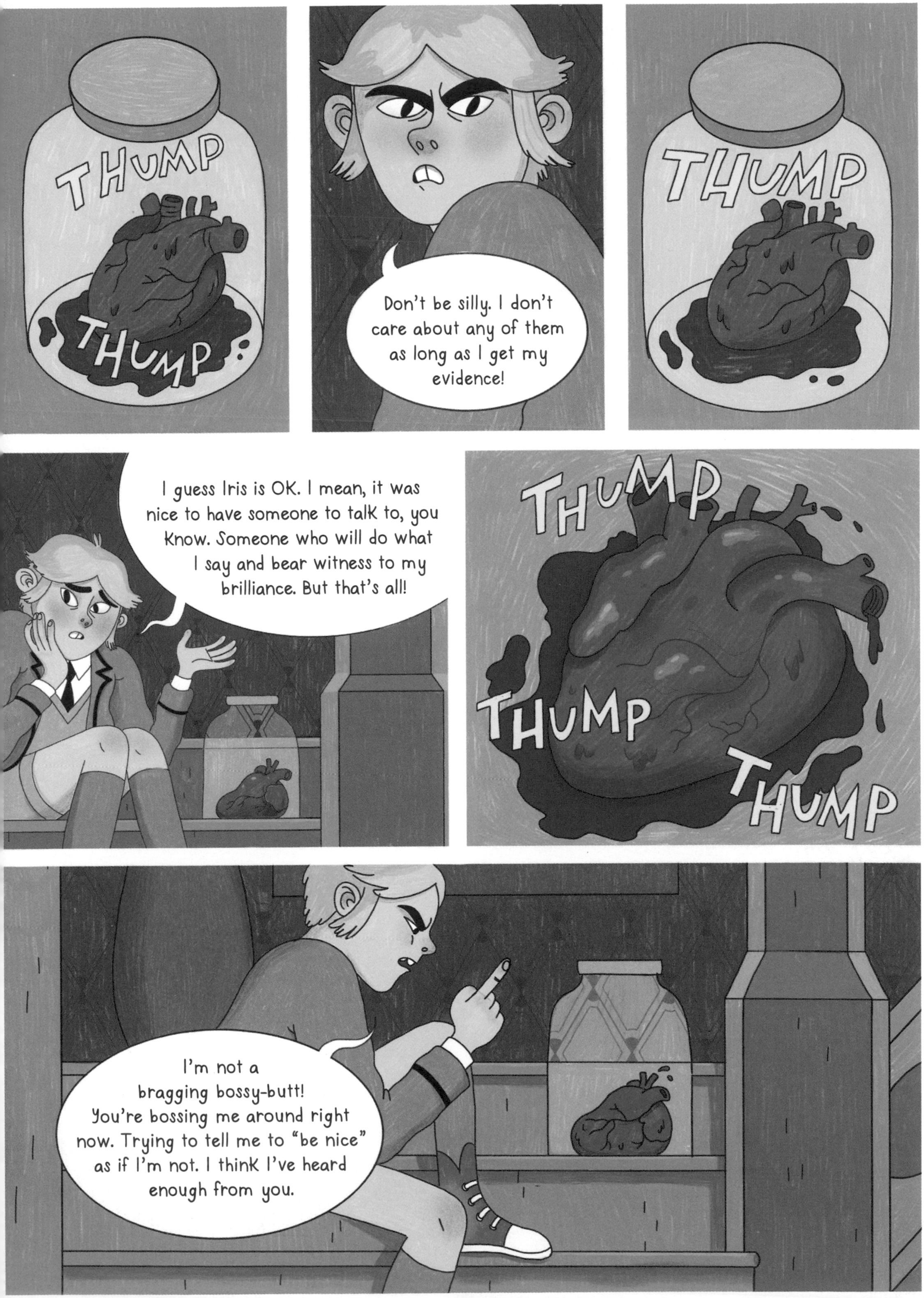
THUMP
THUMP
Don't be silly. I don't care about any of them as long as I get my evidence!
THUMP
I guess Iris is OK. I mean, it was nice to have someone to talk to, you know. Someone who will do what I say and bear witness to my brilliance. But that's all!
THUMP
THUMP
THUMP
I'm not a bragging bossy-butt! You're bossing me around right now. Trying to tell me to "be nice" as if I'm not. I think I've heard enough from you.

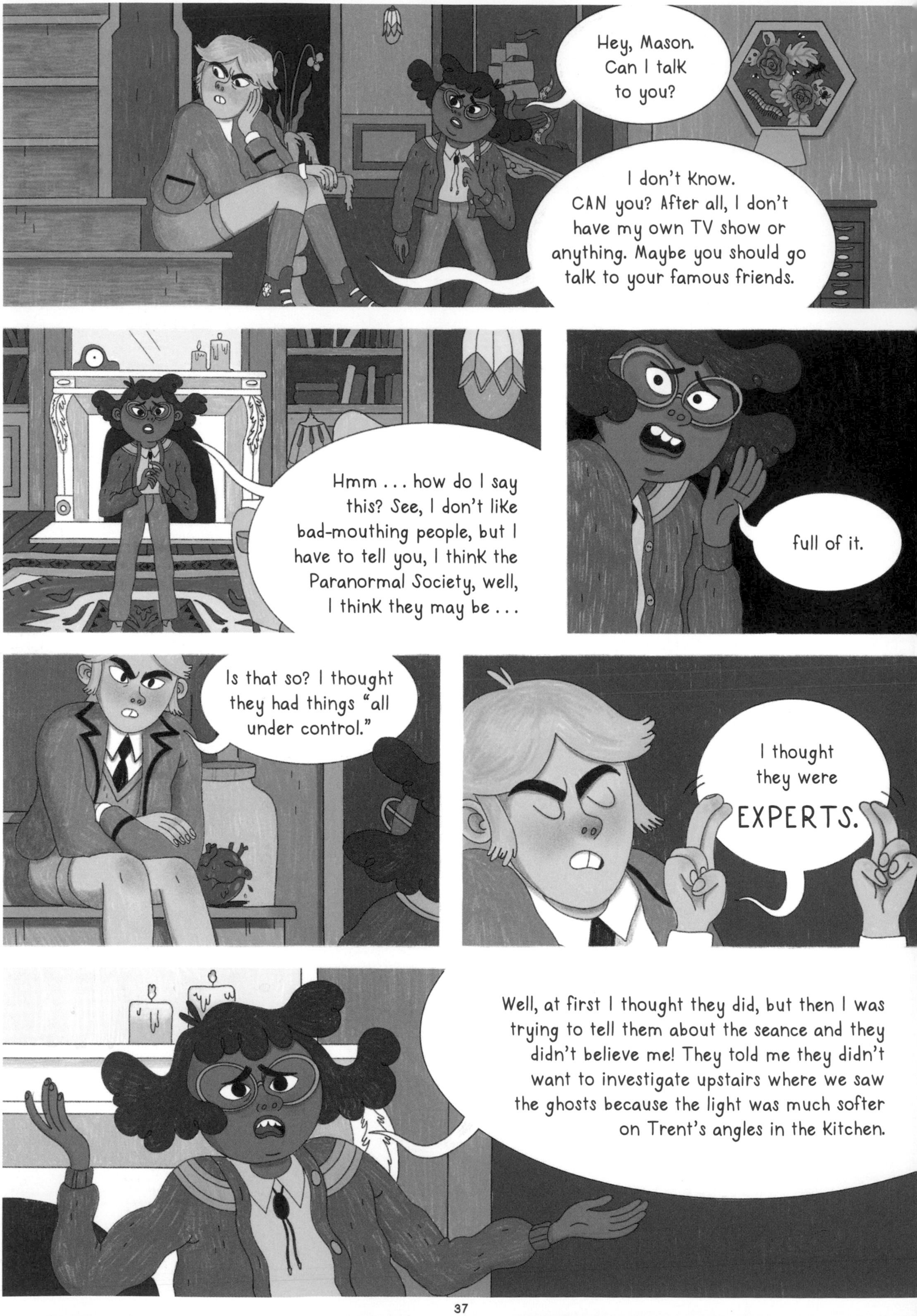
Hey, Mason. Can I talk to you?
I don't know. CAN you? After all, I don't have my own TV show or anything. Maybe you should go talk to your famous friends.
Hmm . . . how do I say this? See, I don't like bad-mouthing people, but I have to tell you, I think the Paranormal Society, well, I think they may be . . .
full of it.
Is that so? I thought they had things "all under control."
I thought they were EXPERTS.
Well, at first I thought they did, but then I was trying to tell them about the seance and they didn't believe me! They told me they didn't want to investigate upstairs where we saw the ghosts because the light was much softer on Trent's angles in the kitchen.

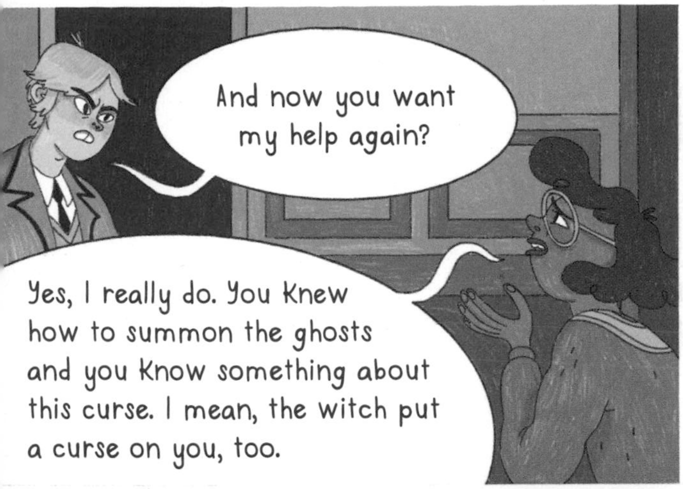
And now you want my help again?
Yes, I really do. You knew how to summon the ghosts and you know something about this curse. I mean, the witch put a curse on you, too.

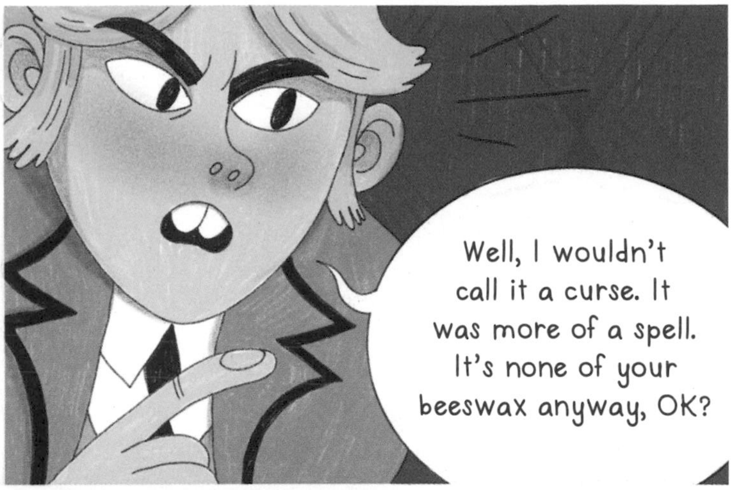
Well, I wouldn't call it a curse. It was more of a spell. It's none of your beeswax anyway, OK?

But Iris was not "OK" with it. She felt that it was indeed some of her "beeswax" and being a particularly inquisitive and determined girl, she refused to give up.

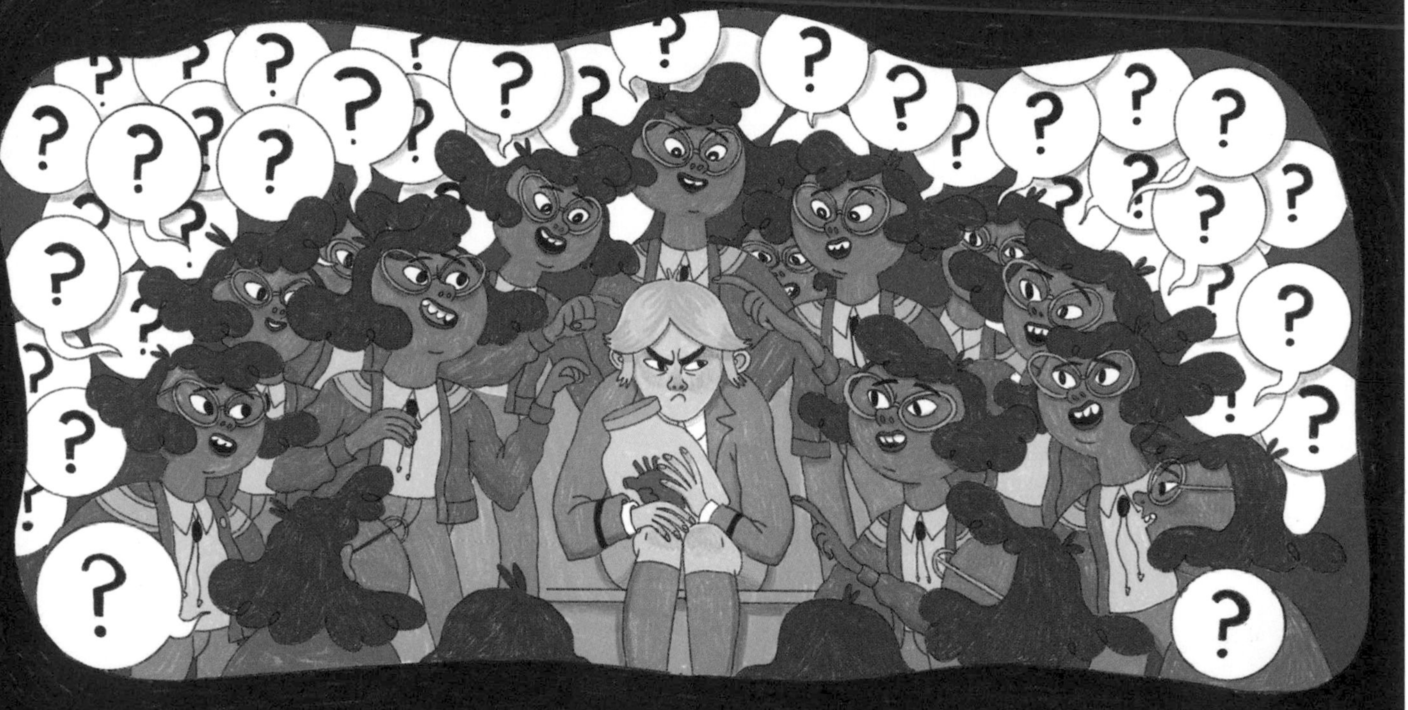

Iris asked Mason to tell her what happened to him exactly two-hundred-twenty-two times before he realized that resistance was futile.

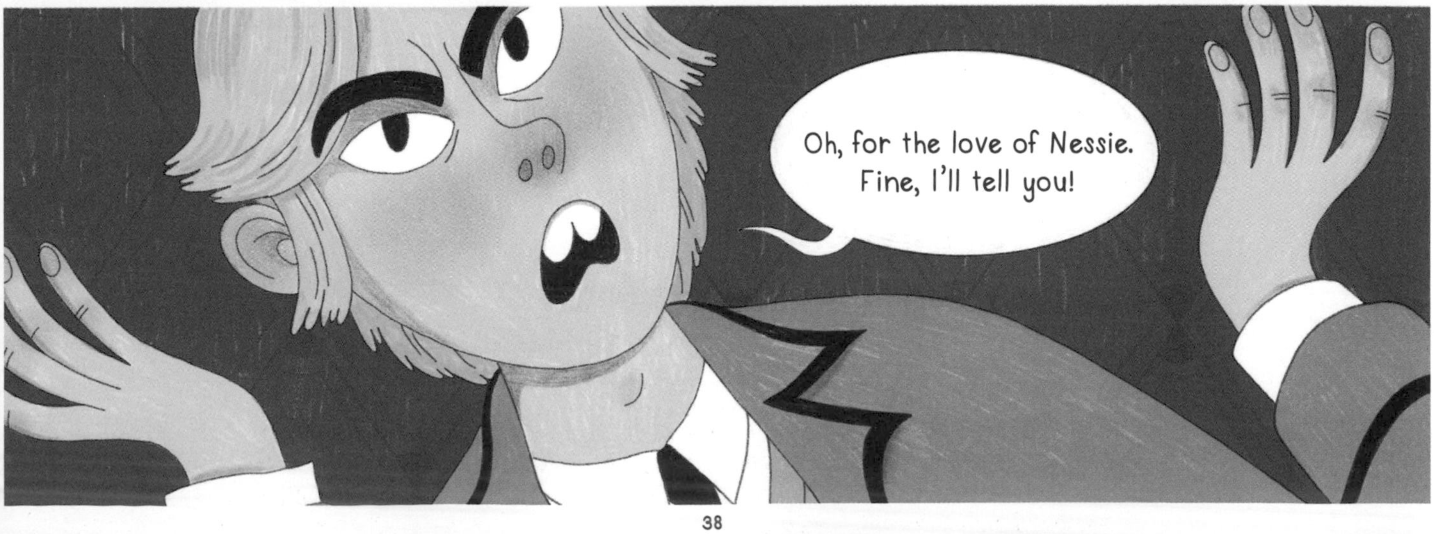
Oh, for the love of Nessie. Fine, I'll tell you!

It all started after I was rejected from the Society. I wanted to be part of their ridiculous team and they called to set me up with an audition. I was to travel to the sand dunes outside of Grimbrook and find the elusive Death Worm.

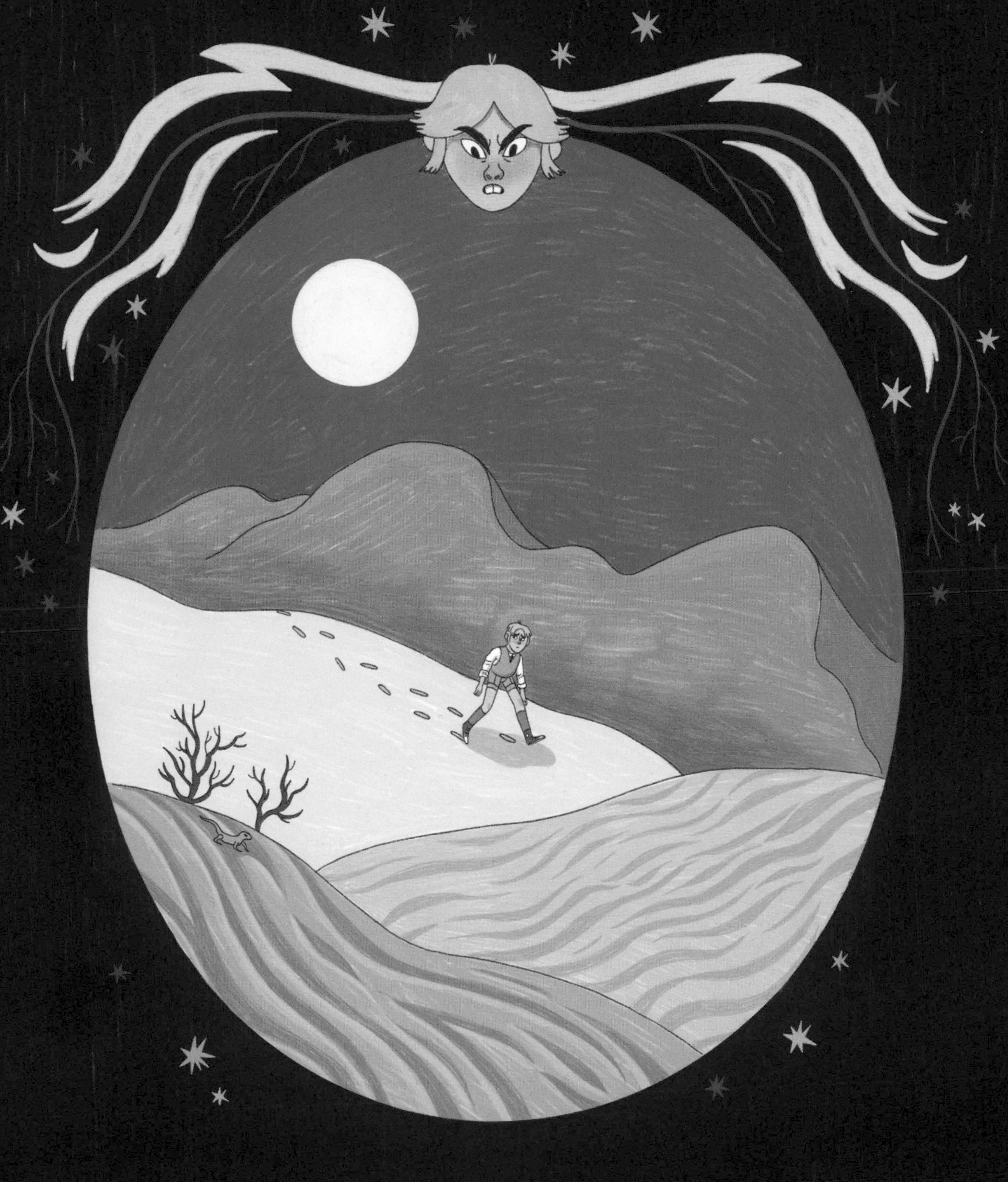

But later I learned that they had no intention of letting me join at all. They didn't even believe the Death Worm existed! It was all just a prank to make fun of me.

The joke was on them though, because I really did find that beastly beast. And boy, oh boy, it's very much real and unspeakably horrible. It has so many teeth... everywhere. And the slime, oh my god, the slime all over its slimy, slimy body... I barely escaped with my life!

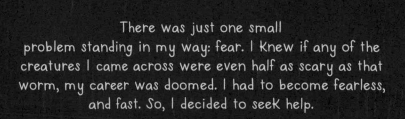

When I returned, I was terrified. But the Society just laughed at me and said I'd let my fear and imagination get the better of me. That's when I vowed to become the best paranormal investigator of all time, to prove to them that not only is the Death Worm real, but other creatures like this really do exist. And many of them are lurking here, in this very town!

There was just one small problem standing in my way: fear. I knew if any of the creatures I came across were even half as scary as that worm, my career was doomed. I had to become fearless, and fast. So, I decided to seek help.

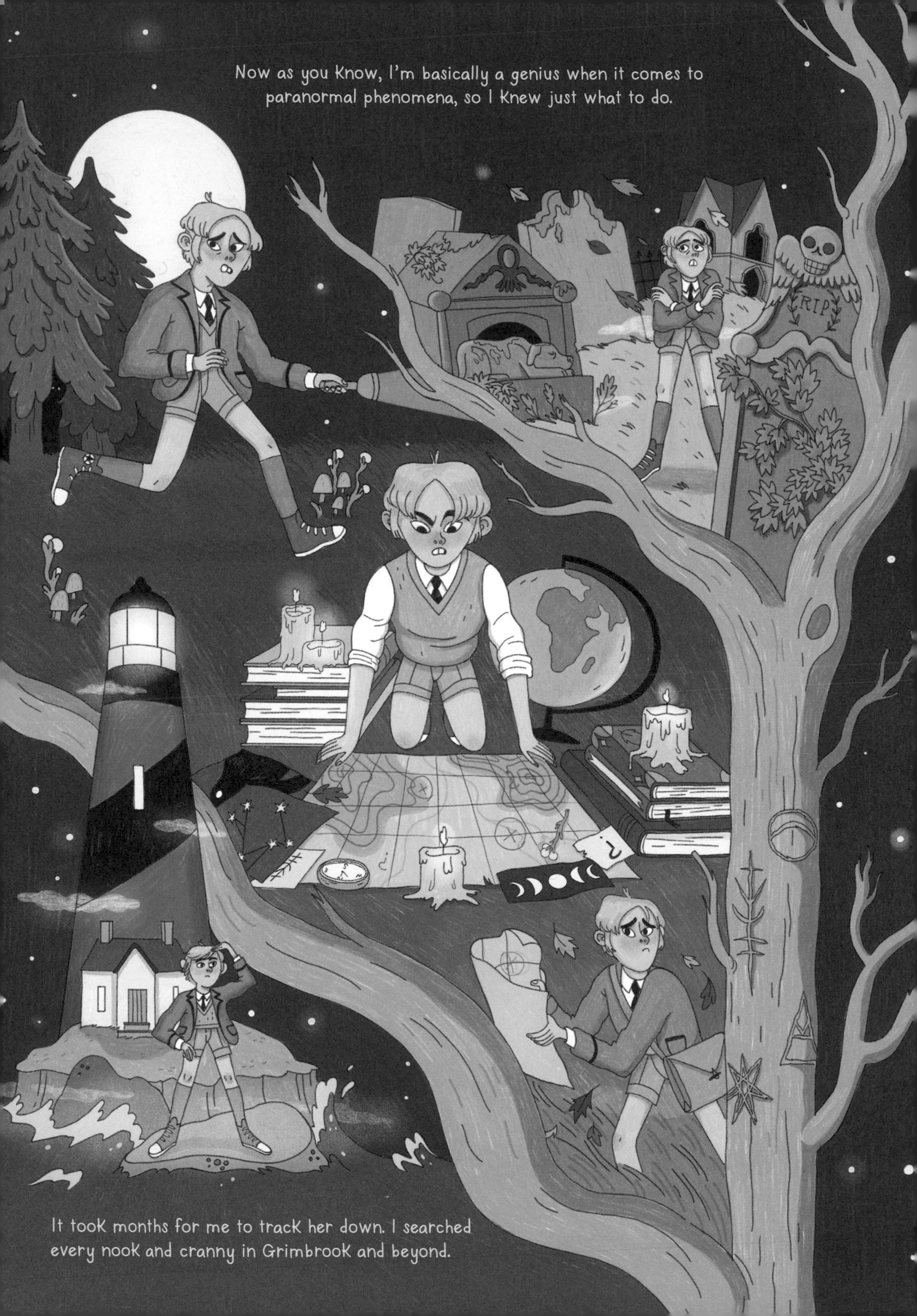

Now as you know, I'm basically a genius when it comes to paranormal phenomena, so I knew just what to do.
RIP
It took months for me to track her down. I searched every nook and cranny in Grimbrook and beyond.

Eventually I found her—Talitha, the witch who some say cursed this town. I mustered up my courage and told her my predicament. At first, she didn't give a rat's tail about it (she was a bit full of herself, actually). It wasn't until I mentioned Trent and his group of phonies, that she changed her tune. I'm not sure what they did to her, but she was keen on revenge in any way possible. So she agreed to help. All I had to do was sign a very simple contract.

So that's what I did.

TERMS & CONDIT
REMOVAL OF FEAR
RESULT IN REMOVAL OF

My heart began to flutter then wham, bam, apple jam—all my fears disappeared!

Admittedly, I had no idea that she was going to remove my ticker for good, but she explained it all in detail afterward.

MASON MOONEY

TERMS & CONDITIONS
REMOVAL OF FEAR MAY
RESULT IN REMOVAL OF

Not that it mattered anyway, I'd got my wish. Now I'm not afraid of anything.

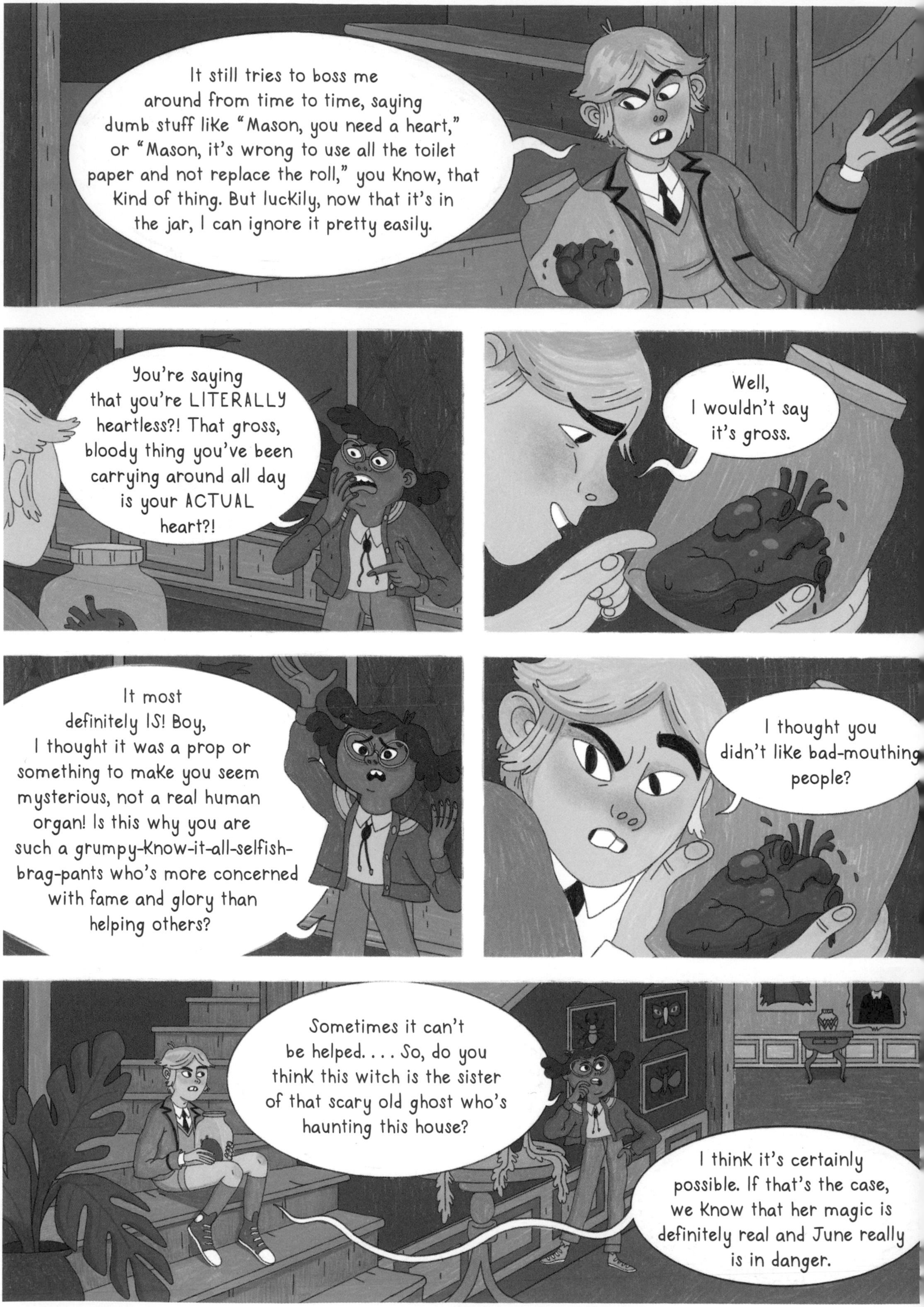
It still tries to boss me around from time to time, saying dumb stuff like "Mason, you need a heart," or "Mason, it's wrong to use all the toilet paper and not replace the roll," you know, that kind of thing. But luckily, now that it's in the jar, I can ignore it pretty easily.
You're saying that you're LITERALLY heartless?! That gross, bloody thing you've been carrying around all day is your ACTUAL heart?!
Well, I wouldn't say it's gross.
It most definitely IS! Boy, I thought it was a prop or something to make you seem mysterious, not a real human organ! Is this why you are such a grumpy-know-it-all-selfish-brag-pants who's more concerned with fame and glory than helping others?
I thought you didn't like bad-mouthing people?
Sometimes it can't be helped. . . . So, do you think this witch is the sister of that scary old ghost who's haunting this house?
I think it's certainly possible. If that's the case, we know that her magic is definitely real and June really is in danger.

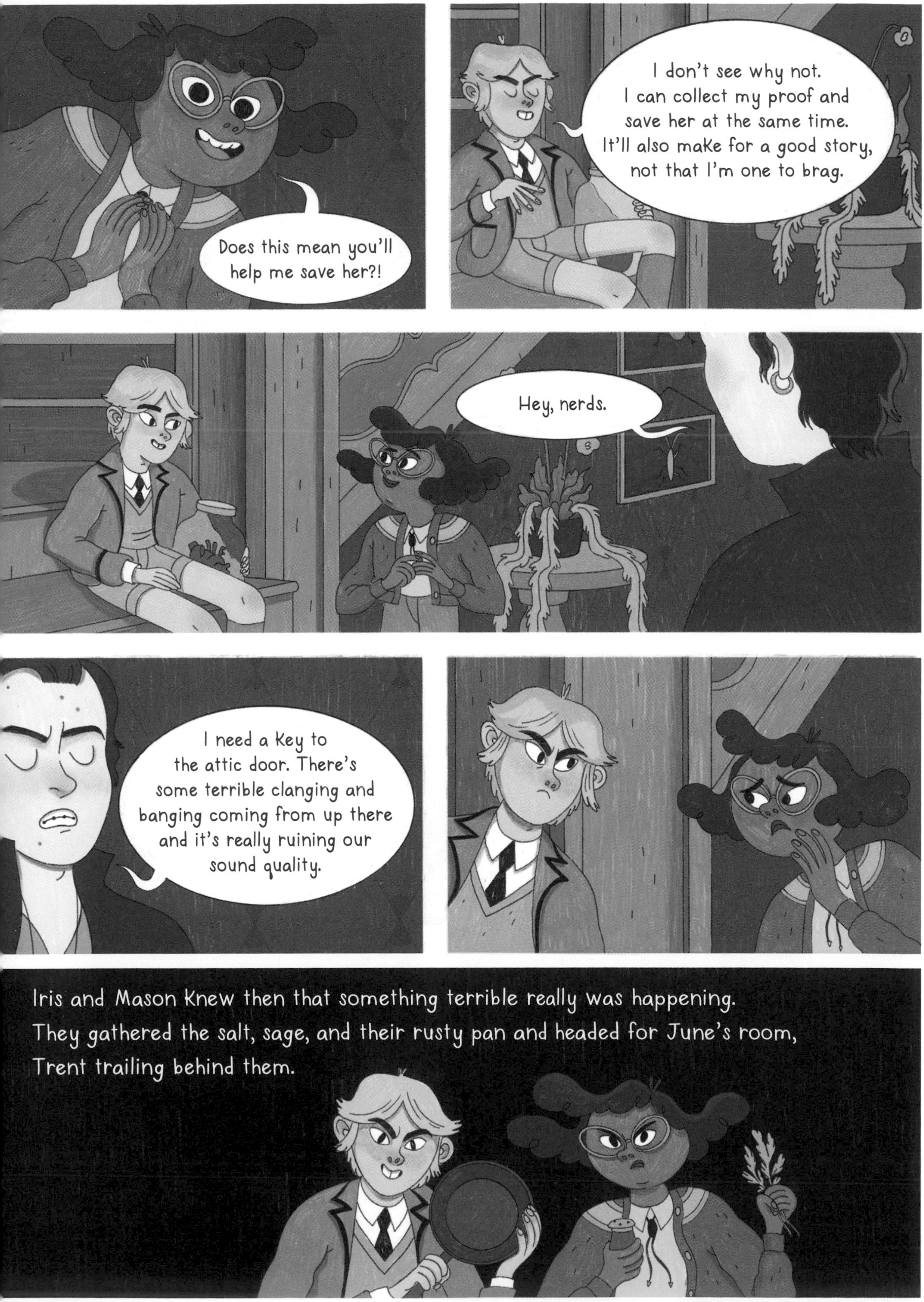
Does this mean you'll help me save her?!
I don't see why not. I can collect my proof and save her at the same time. It'll also make for a good story, not that I'm one to brag.
Hey, nerds.
I need a key to the attic door. There's some terrible clanging and banging coming from up there and it's really ruining our sound quality.
Iris and Mason knew then that something terrible really was happening. They gathered the salt, sage, and their rusty pan and headed for June's room, Trent trailing behind them.

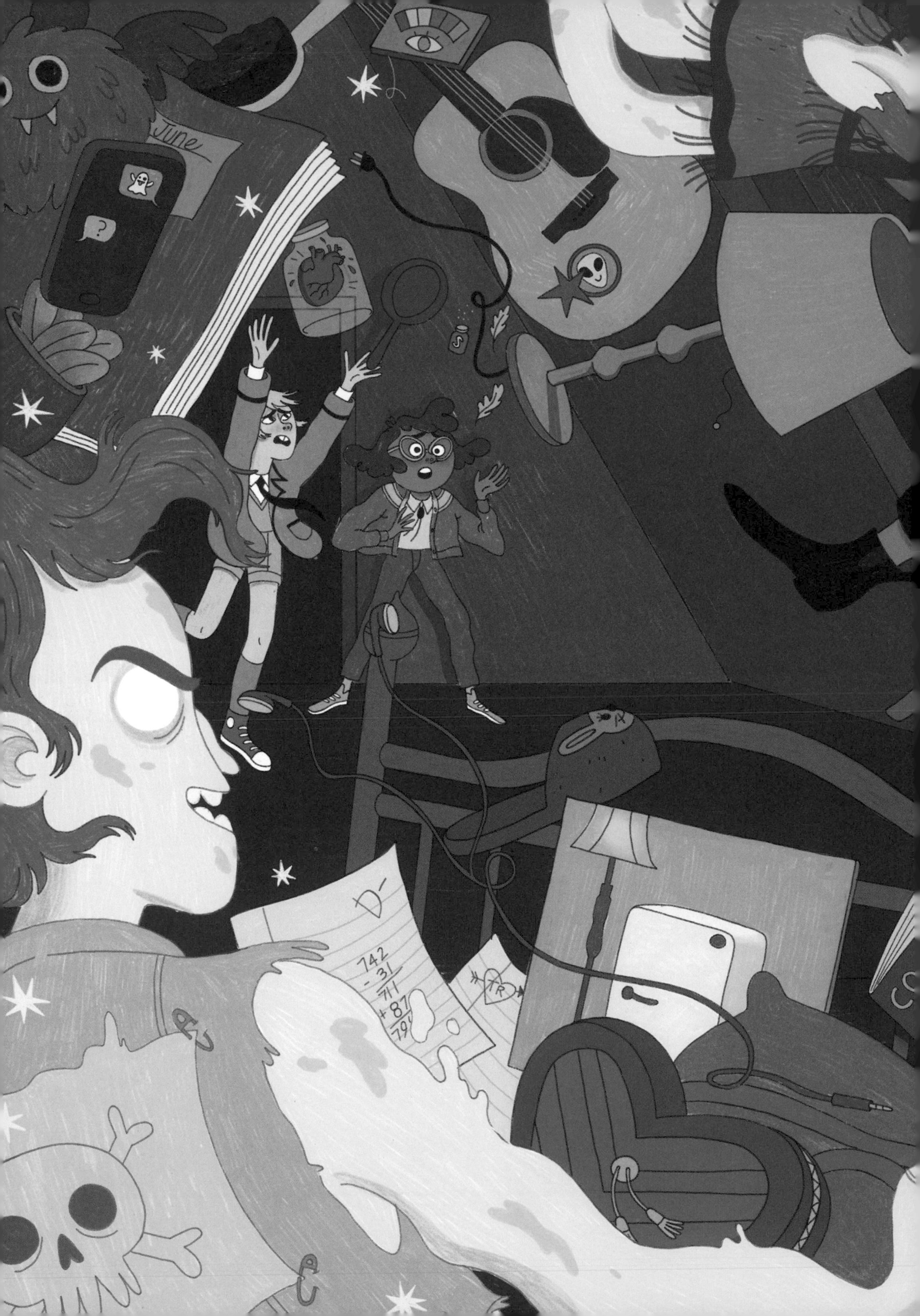
June
742
- 31
711
+ 87

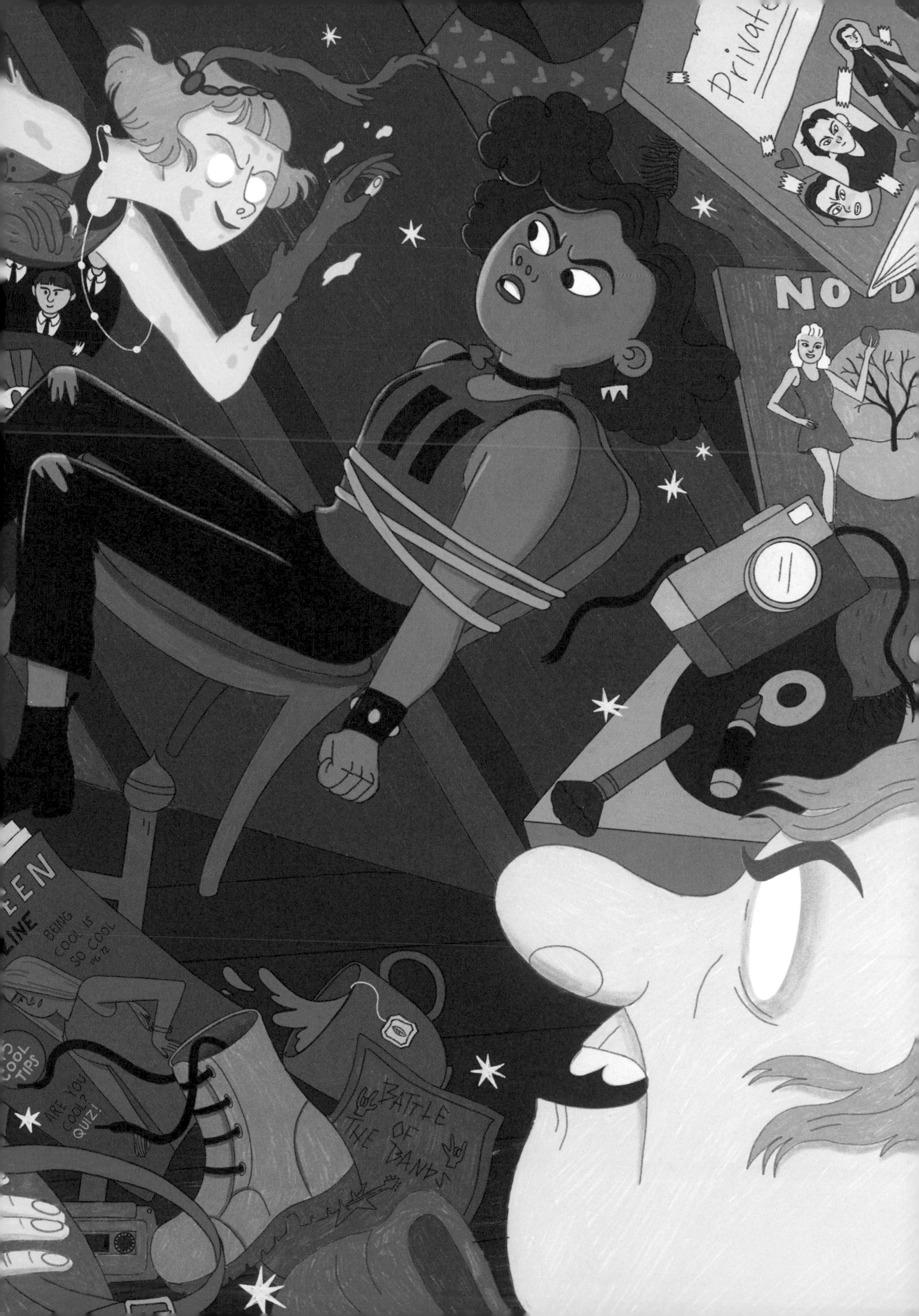
Private
BEING COOL IS SO COOL
ARE YOU COOL? QUIZ!
BATTLE OF THE BANDS

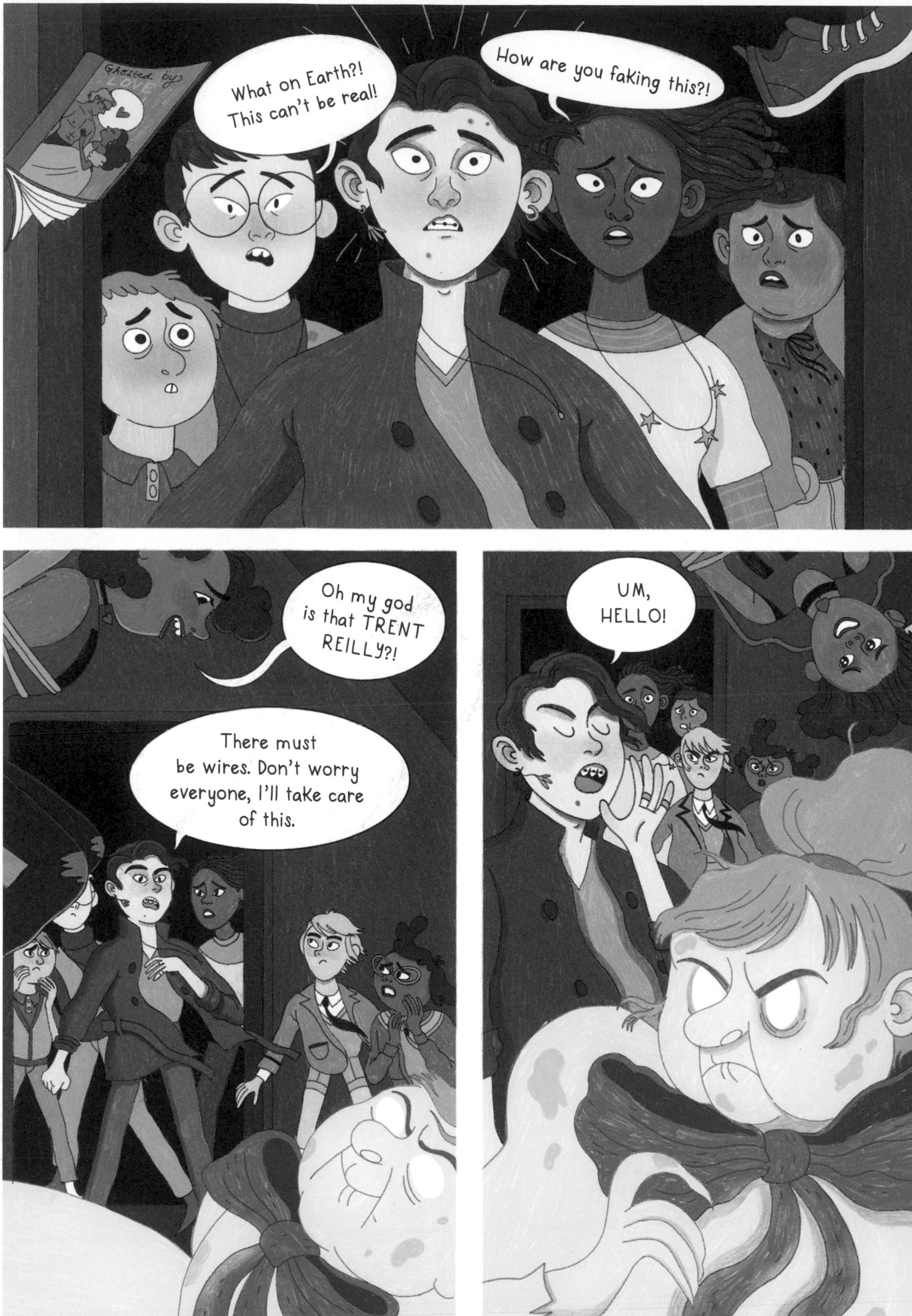
Ghosted by LOVE
What on Earth?! This can't be real!
How are you faking this?!
Oh my god is that TRENT REILLY?!
There must be wires. Don't worry everyone, I'll take care of this.
UM, HELLO!

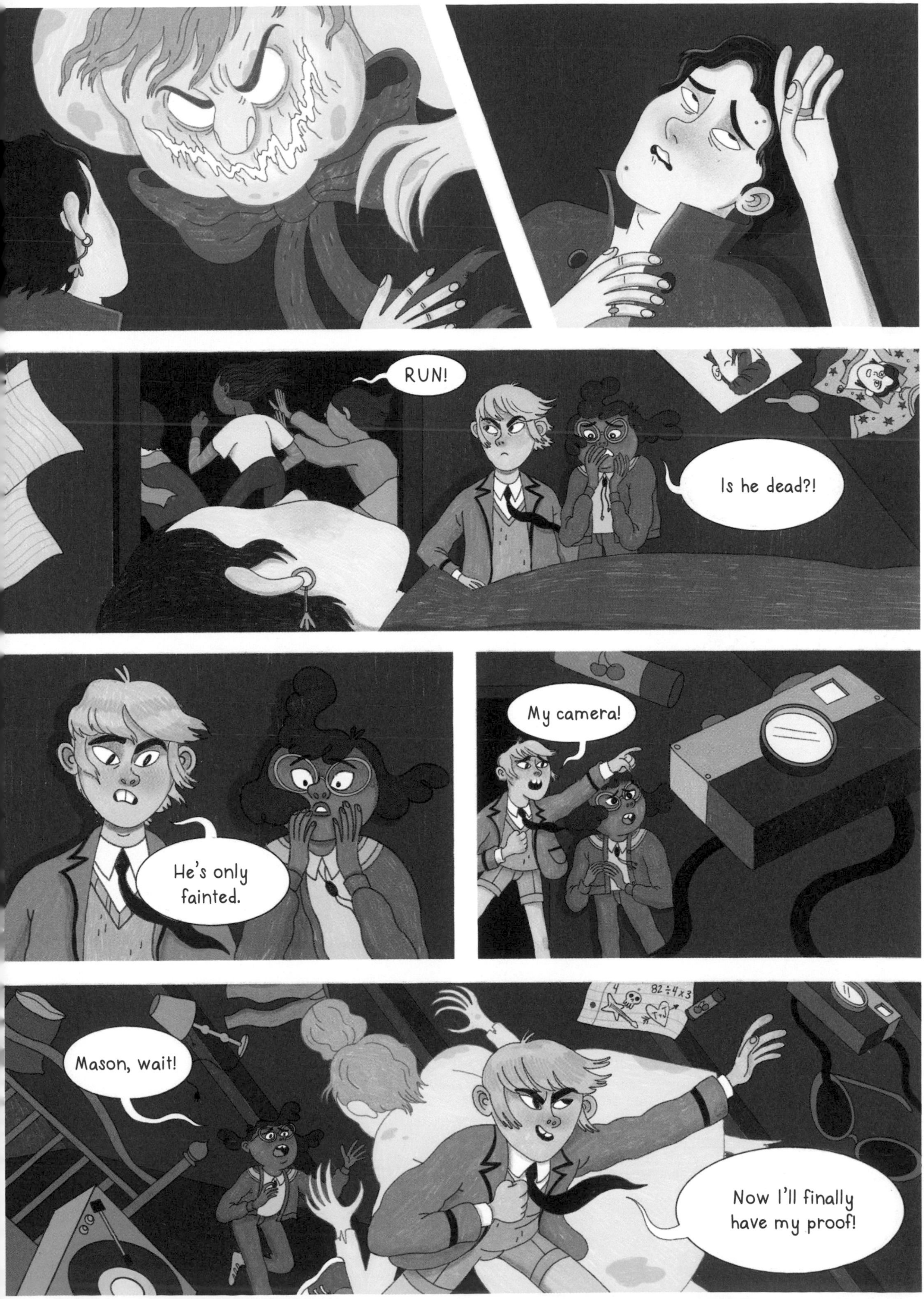
RUN!
Is he dead?!
He's only fainted.
My camera!
Mason, wait!
Now I'll finally have my proof!

While Mason scrambled for his camera, Iris had other things to worry about. . . .

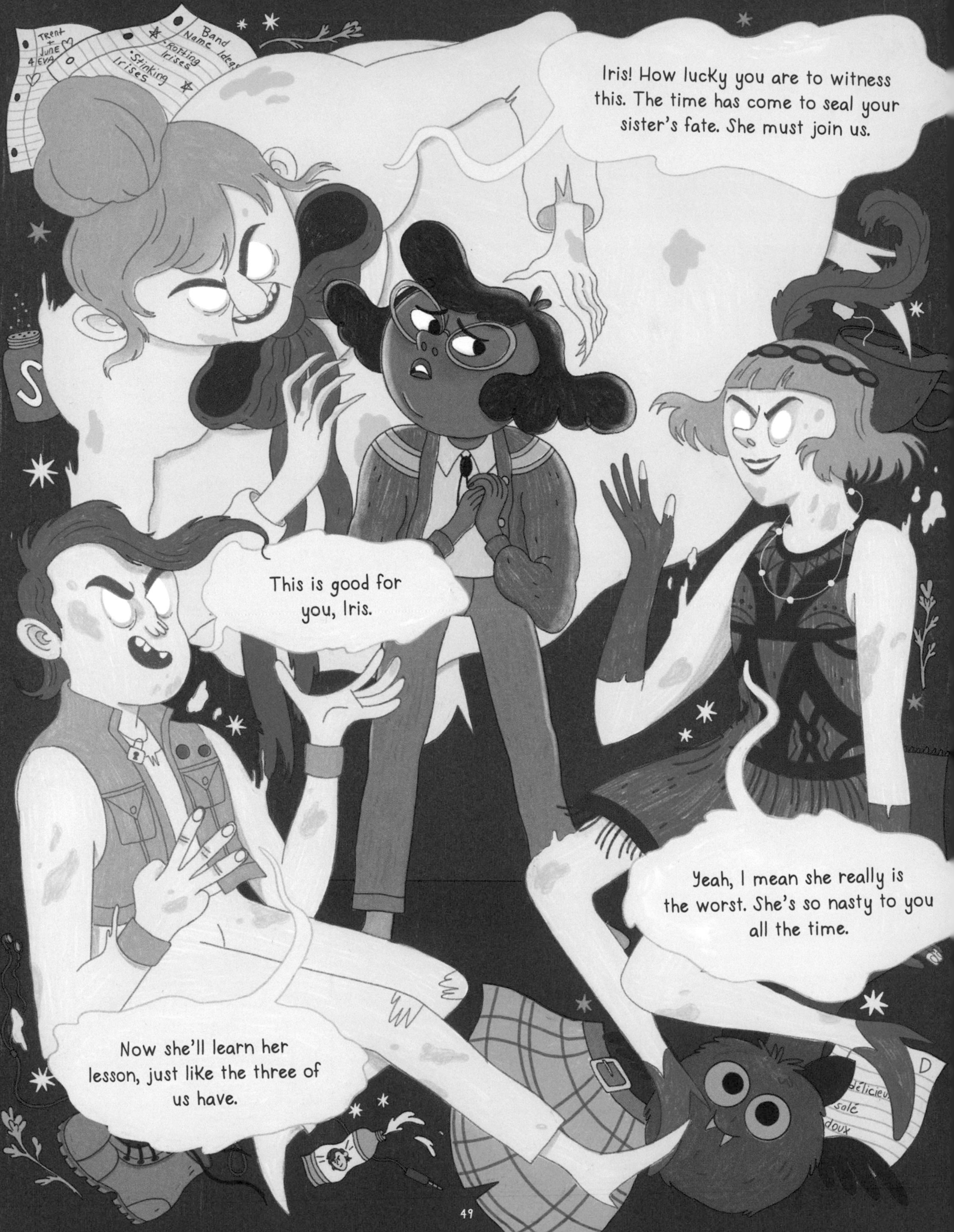

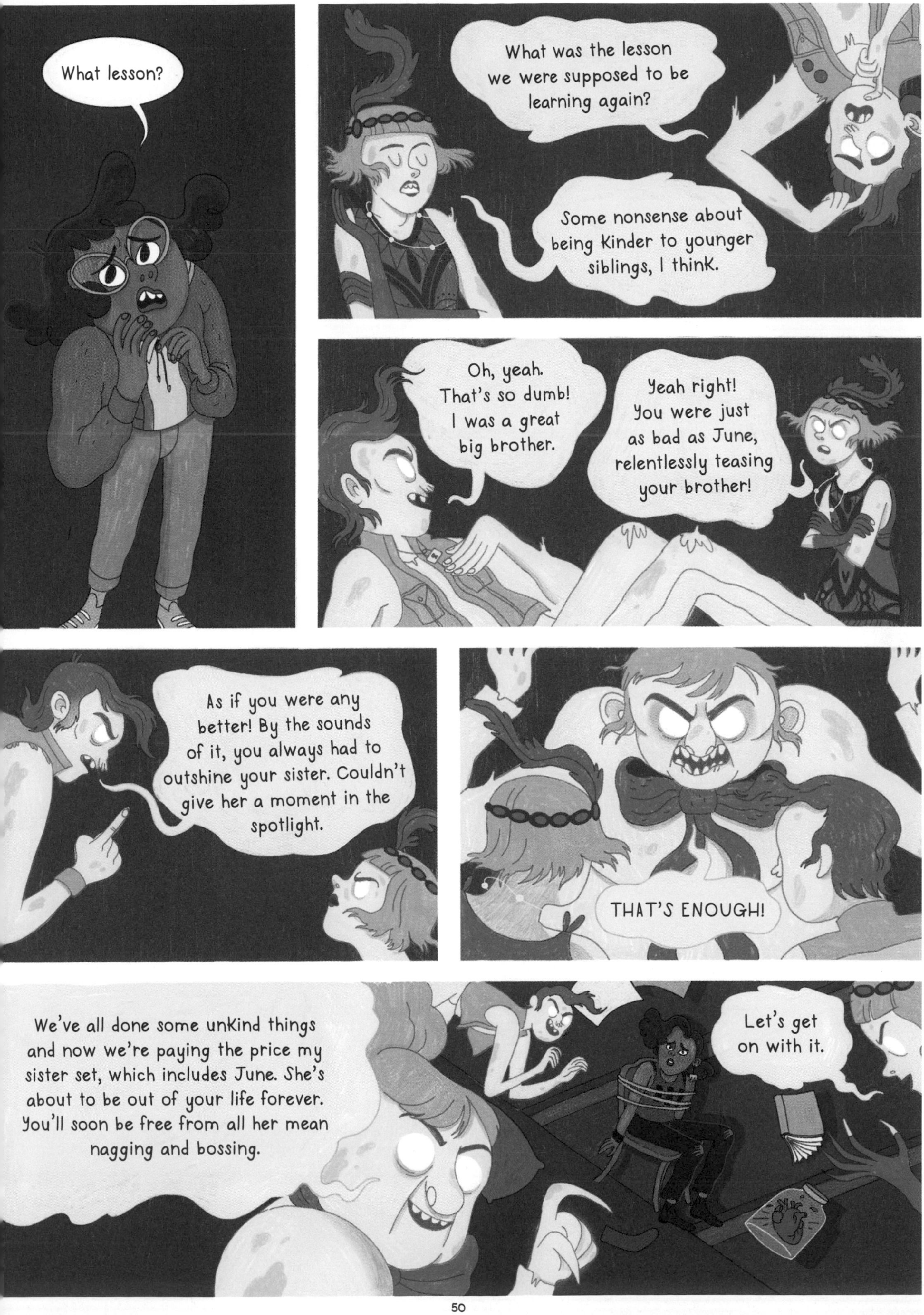
What lesson?
What was the lesson we were supposed to be learning again?
Some nonsense about being kinder to younger siblings, I think.
Oh, yeah. That's so dumb! I was a great big brother.
Yeah right! You were just as bad as June, relentlessly teasing your brother!
As if you were any better! By the sounds of it, you always had to outshine your sister. Couldn't give her a moment in the spotlight.
THAT'S ENOUGH!
We've all done some unkind things and now we're paying the price my sister set, which includes June. She's about to be out of your life forever. You'll soon be free from all her mean nagging and bossing.
Let's get on with it.

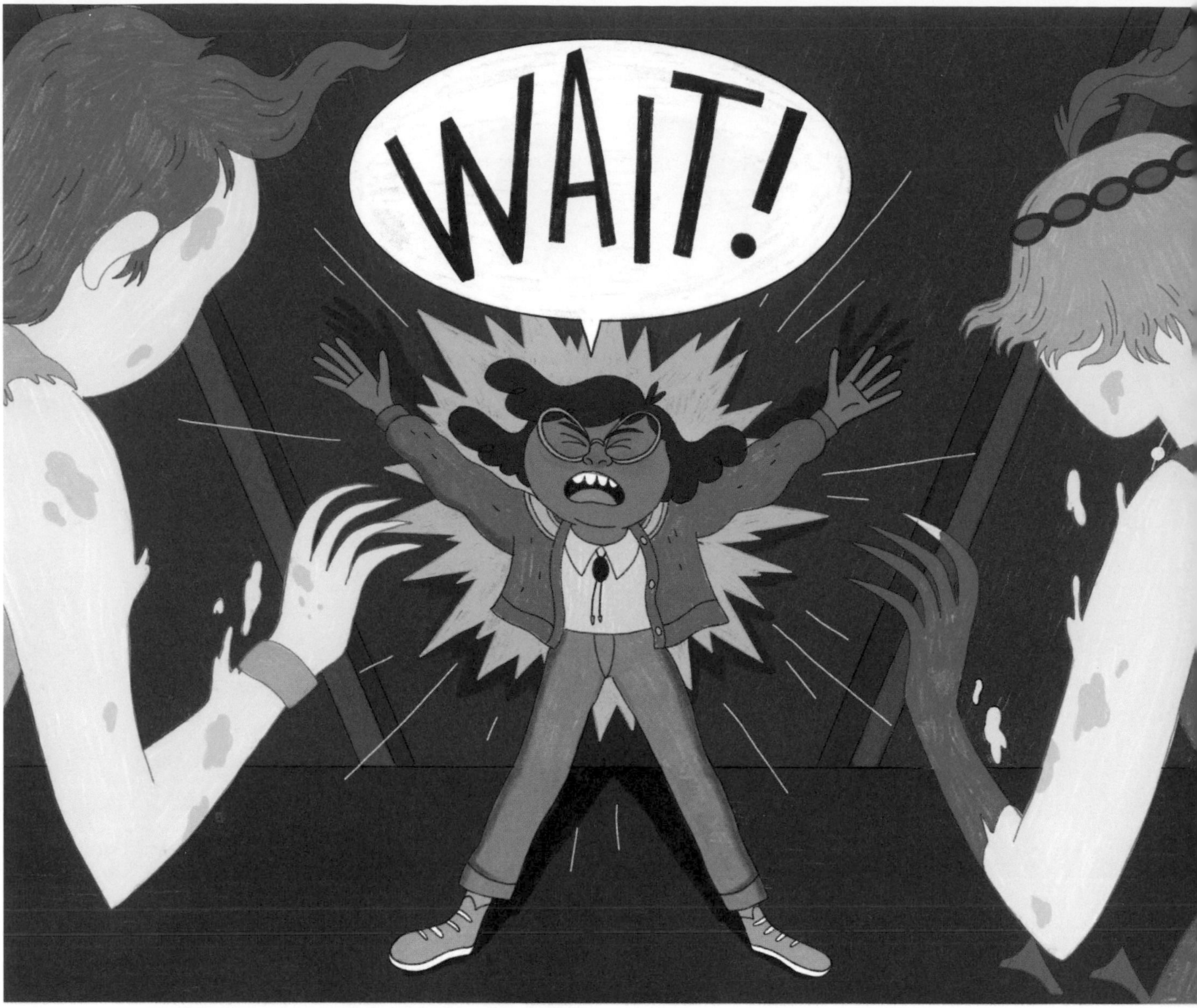
WAIT!

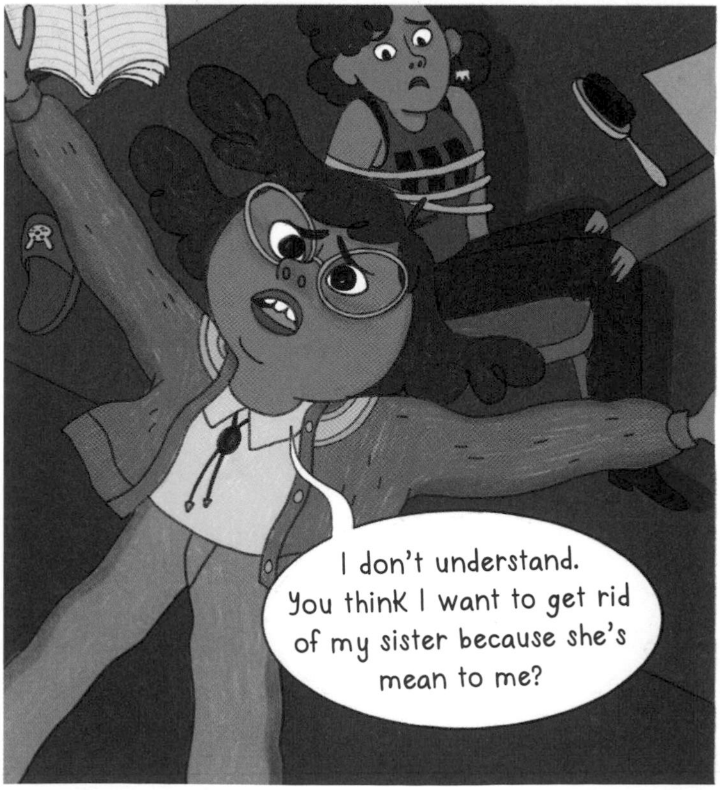
I don't understand. You think I want to get rid of my sister because she's mean to me?

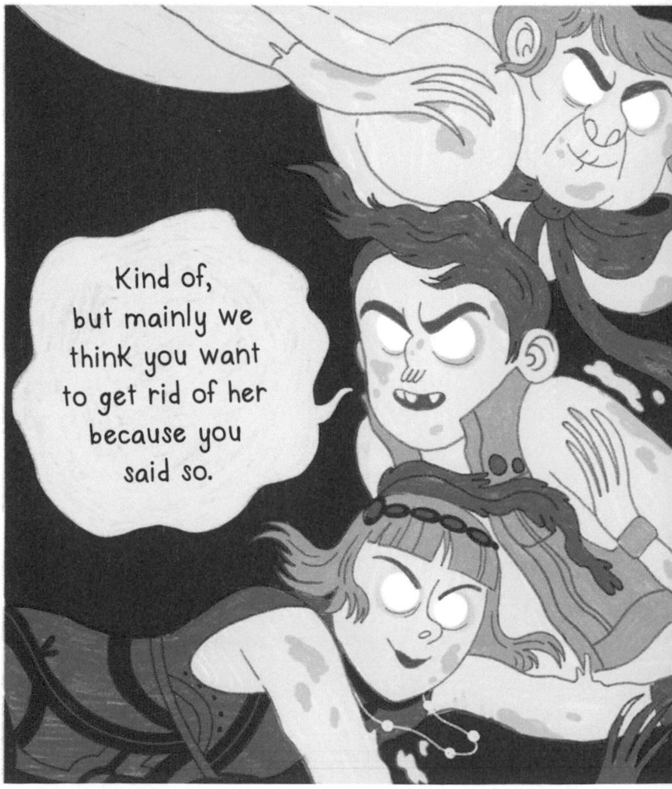
Kind of, but mainly we think you want to get rid of her because you said so.

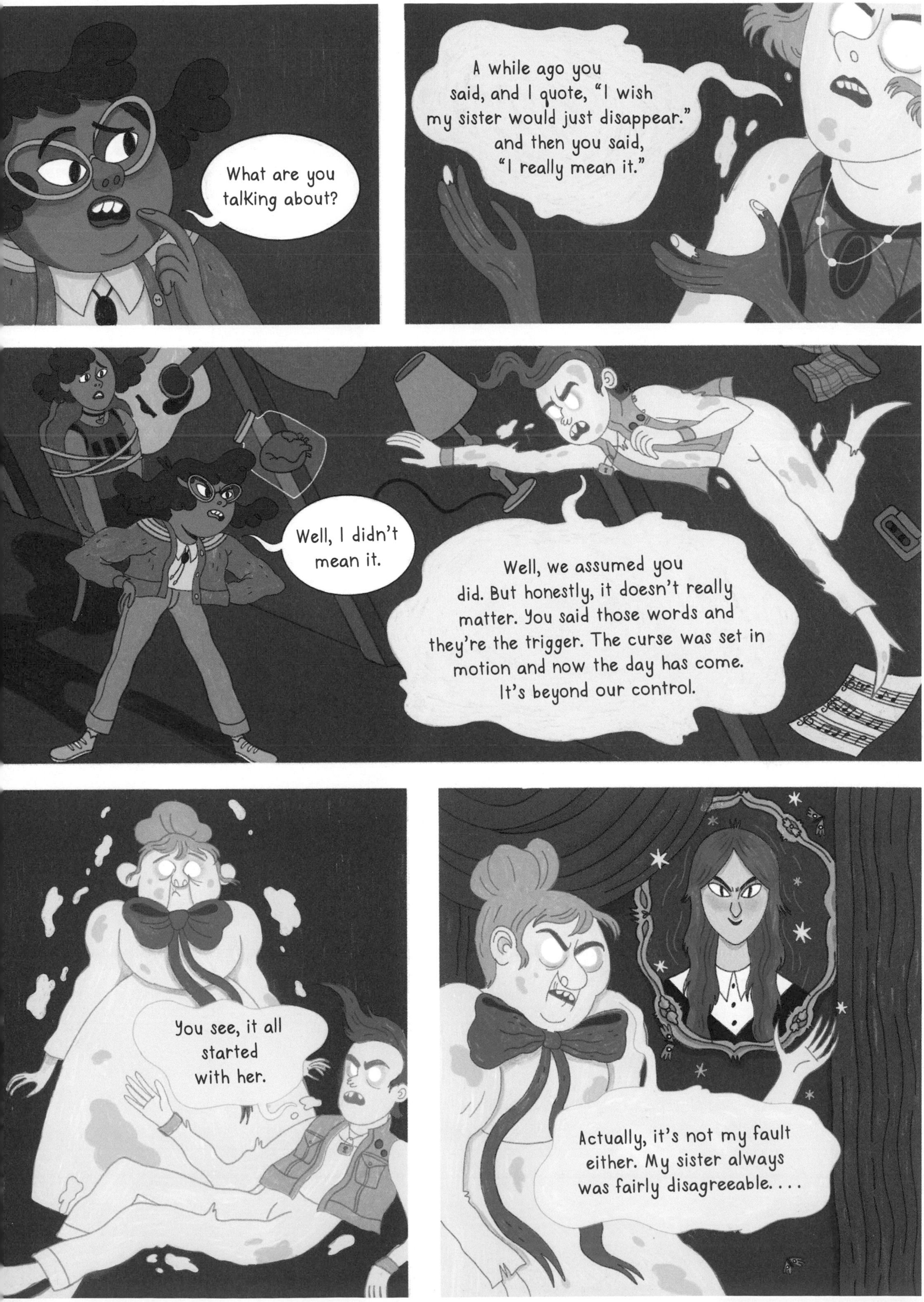

What are you talking about?
A while ago you said, and I quote, "I wish my sister would just disappear." and then you said, "I really mean it."
Well, I didn't mean it.
Well, we assumed you did. But honestly, it doesn't really matter. You said those words and they're the trigger. The curse was set in motion and now the day has come. It's beyond our control.
You see, it all started with her.
Actually, it's not my fault either. My sister always was fairly disagreeable. . . .

Instead of doing needlepoint and practicing piano, she was always asking questions and reading the most peculiar books. She was so different to other girls our age and since we lived together everyone thought I was strange, too. People began to refer to us as "the spinster sisters."

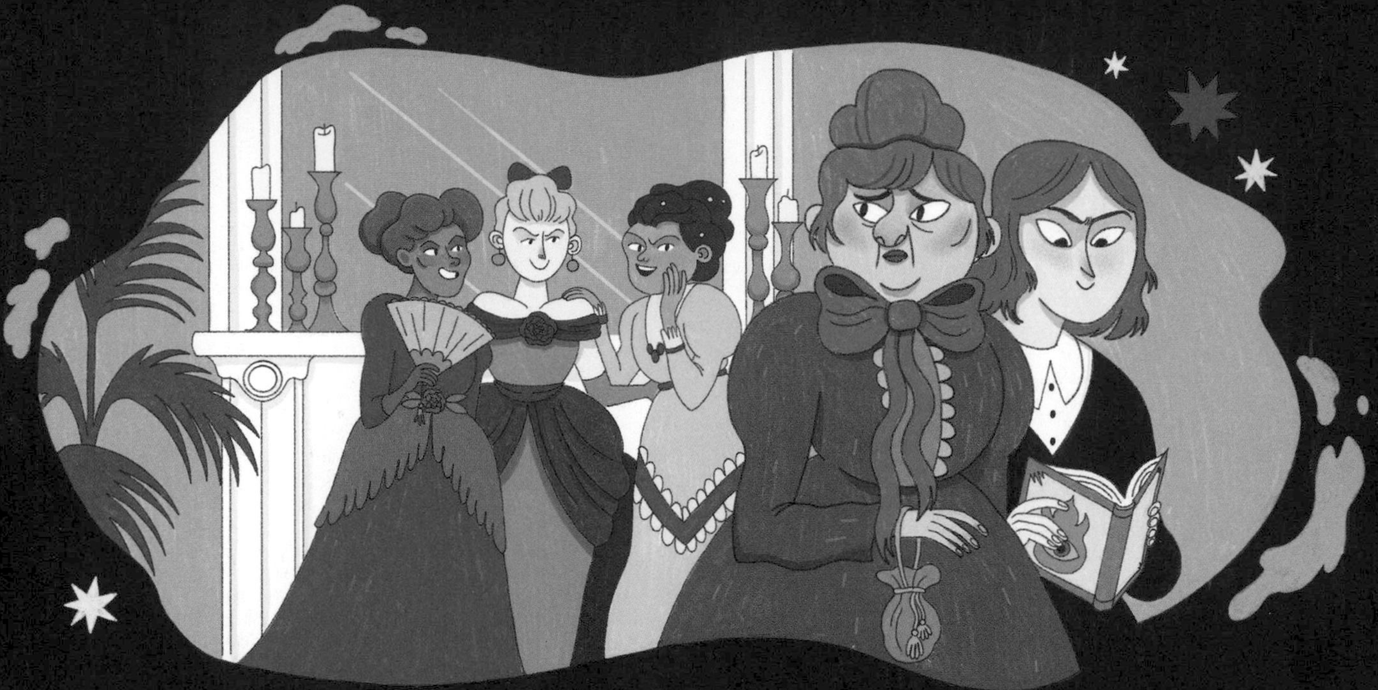

What she needed was some good bossing and as the older sibling that was my job. I really tried. I threw away her books, but she just found even stranger ones to read.

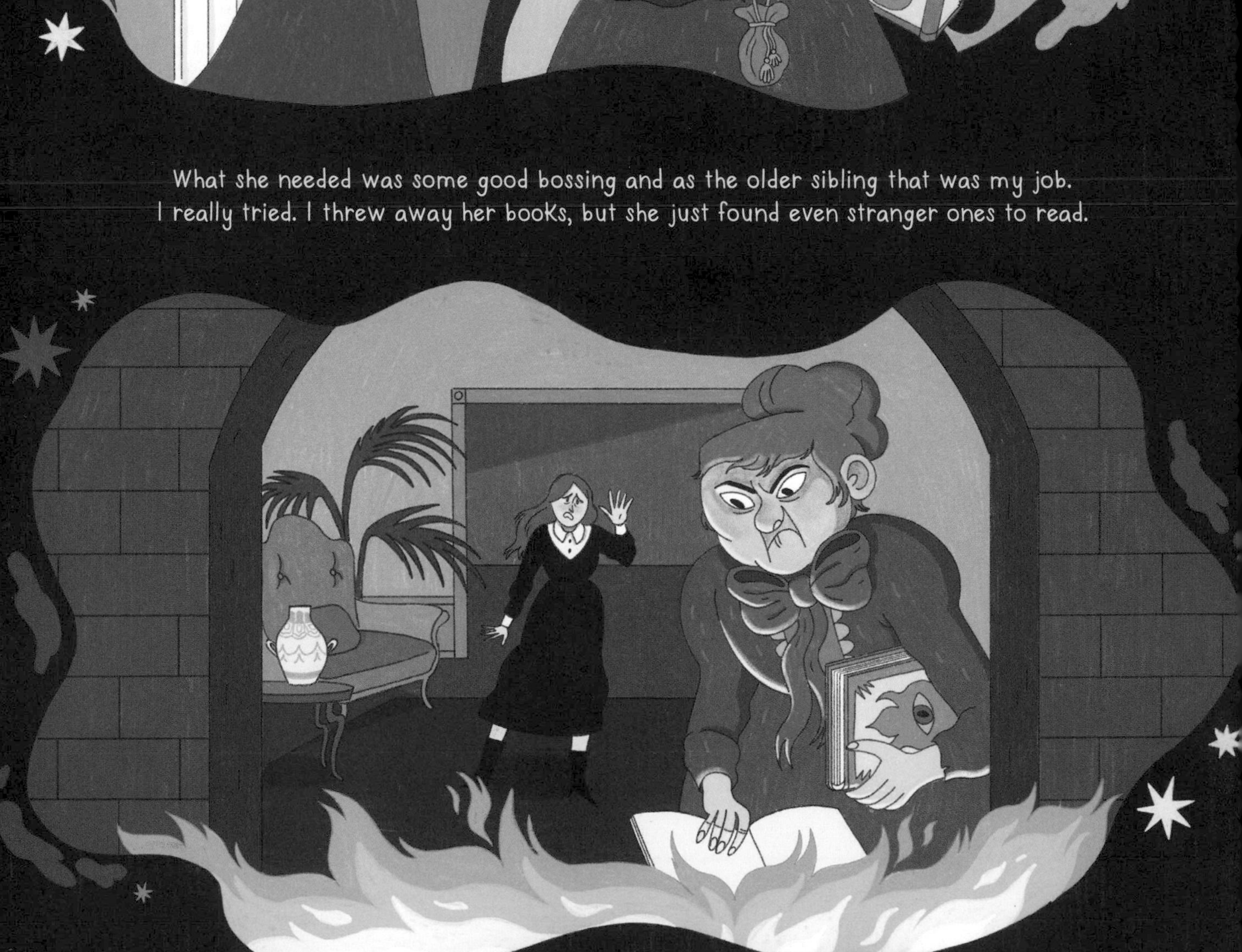

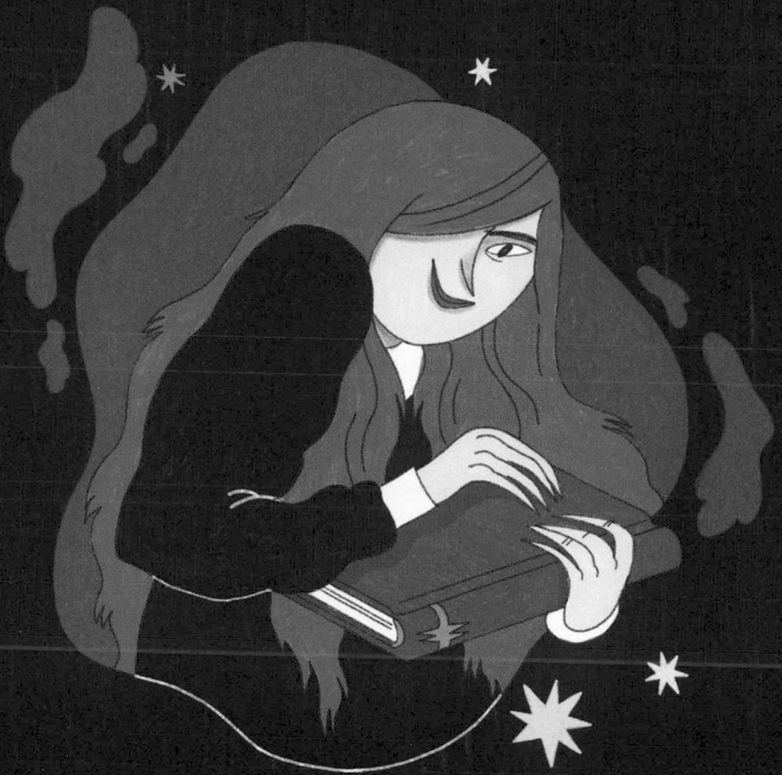

As the years went by, she became more perplexing and I grew more frustrated. In her quest for other unusual things to read, she discovered a very curious book indeed. Upon finishing it, she was altogether different. She seemed to possess something unworldly and unsettling.

She started to sneak up behind me and stare blankly. I found it a little unnerving, to say the least. Normally she would leave if I told her to, until one day. . . .

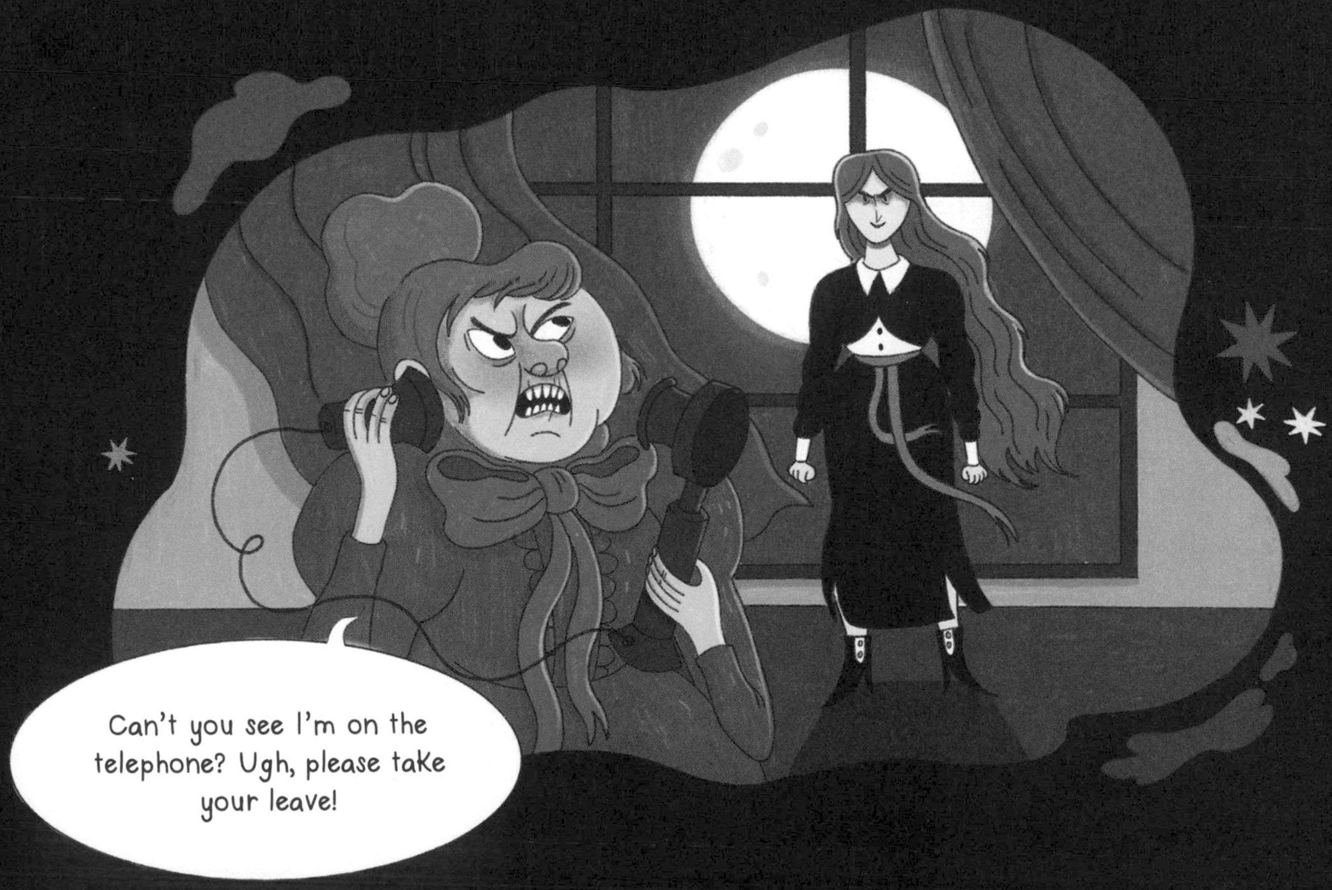
Can't you see I'm on the telephone? Ugh, please take your leave!

But this time, she didn't leave. She just stood there and smiled. I don't really understand what happened next. . . .

It was as if my body was gone, but I was still there. When I tried to drink my cup of tea, it poured right through me and onto the floor. When I tried to leave the house, it felt as though an invisible force was blocking the door. The next morning, my sister was gone and all she left behind was a note.

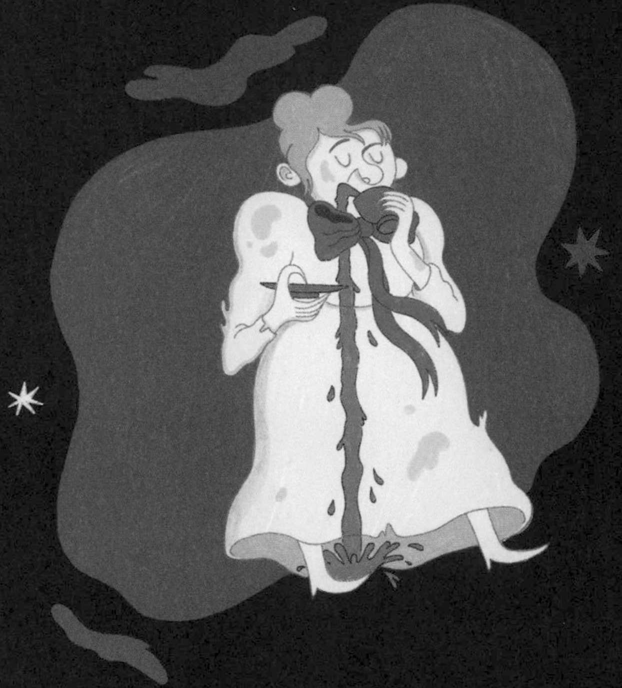

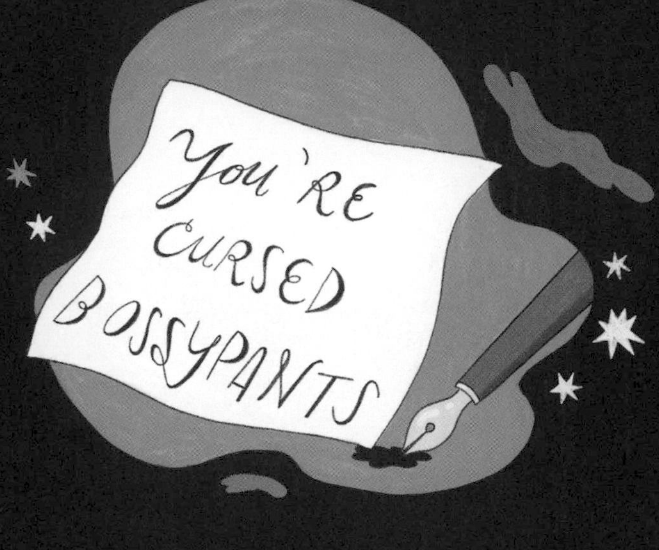
YOU'RE CURSED BOSSYPANTS

And that was that. I was alone in this house for many years, until Ida's family moved in. They couldn't see me, but I watched them. Ida was terrible to her sister, jealous and mean.

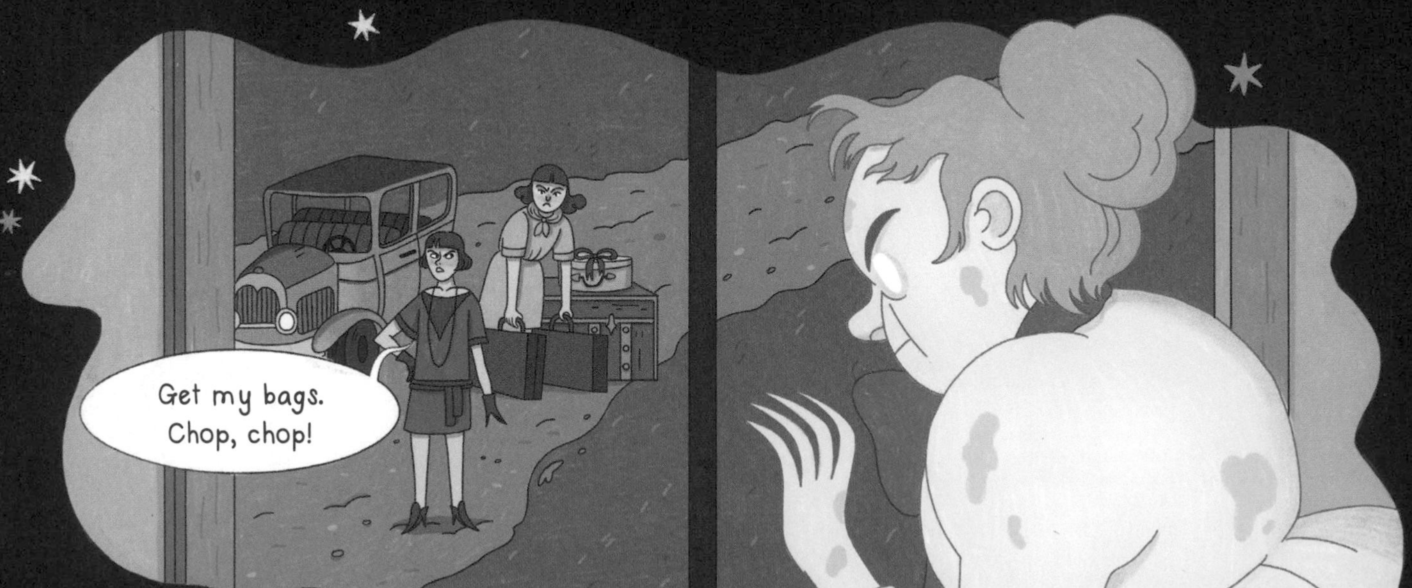
Get my bags. Chop, chop!

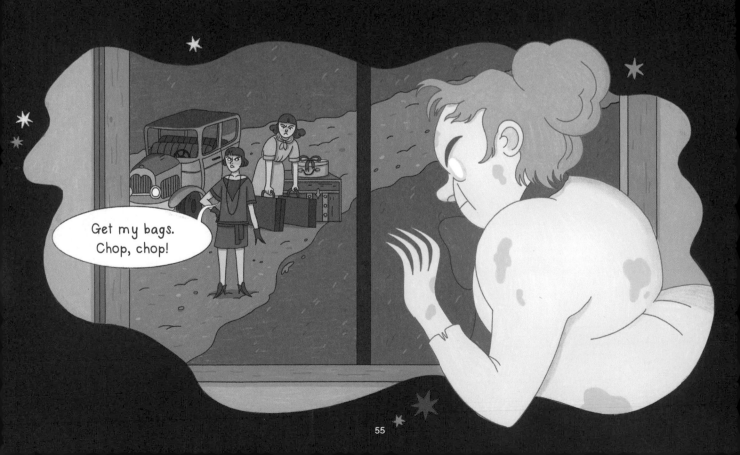

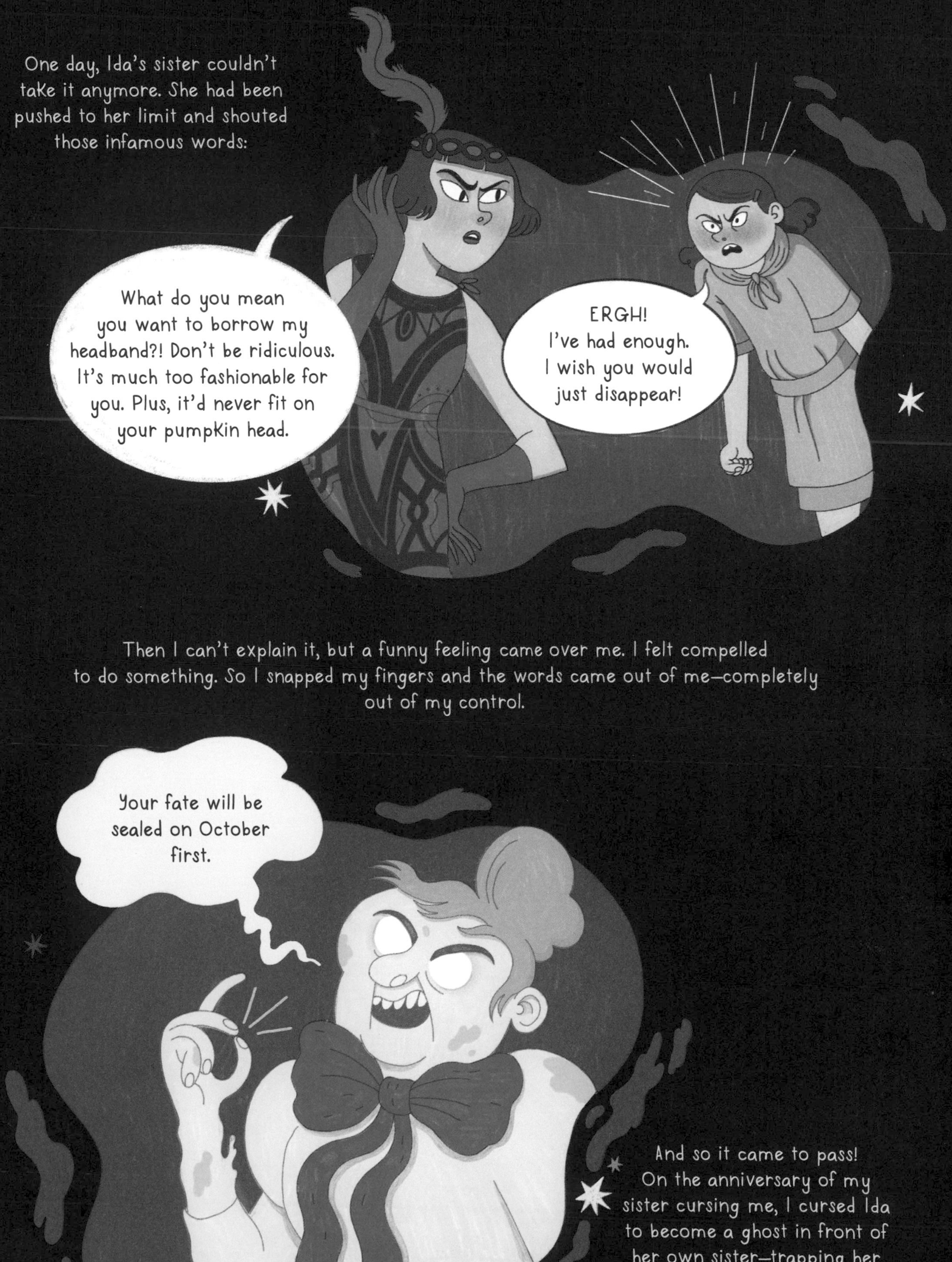
One day, Ida's sister couldn't take it anymore. She had been pushed to her limit and shouted those infamous words:
What do you mean you want to borrow my headband?! Don't be ridiculous. It's much too fashionable for you. Plus, it'd never fit on your pumpkin head.
ERGH! I've had enough. I wish you would just disappear!
Then I can't explain it, but a funny feeling came over me. I felt compelled to do something. So I snapped my fingers and the words came out of me—completely out of my control.
Your fate will be sealed on October first.
And so it came to pass! On the anniversary of my sister cursing me, I cursed Ida to become a ghost in front of her own sister—trapping her in this house for eternity.

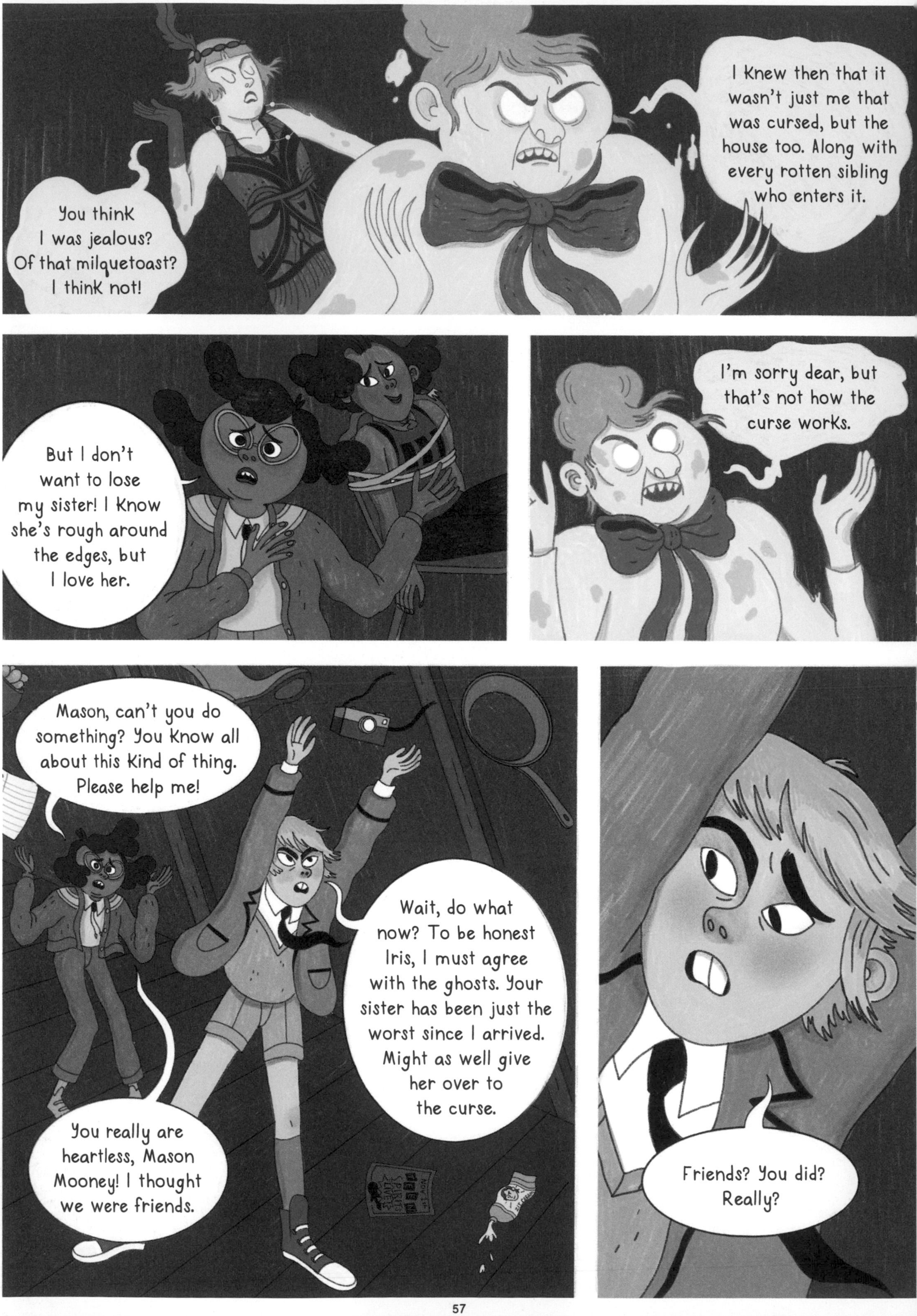
You think I was jealous? Of that milquetoast? I think not!
I knew then that it wasn't just me that was cursed, but the house too. Along with every rotten sibling who enters it.
But I don't want to lose my sister! I know she's rough around the edges, but I love her.
I'm sorry dear, but that's not how the curse works.
Mason, can't you do something? You know all about this kind of thing. Please help me!
Wait, do what now? To be honest Iris, I must agree with the ghosts. Your sister has been just the worst since I arrived. Might as well give her over to the curse.
You really are heartless, Mason Mooney! I thought we were friends.
Friends? You did? Really?

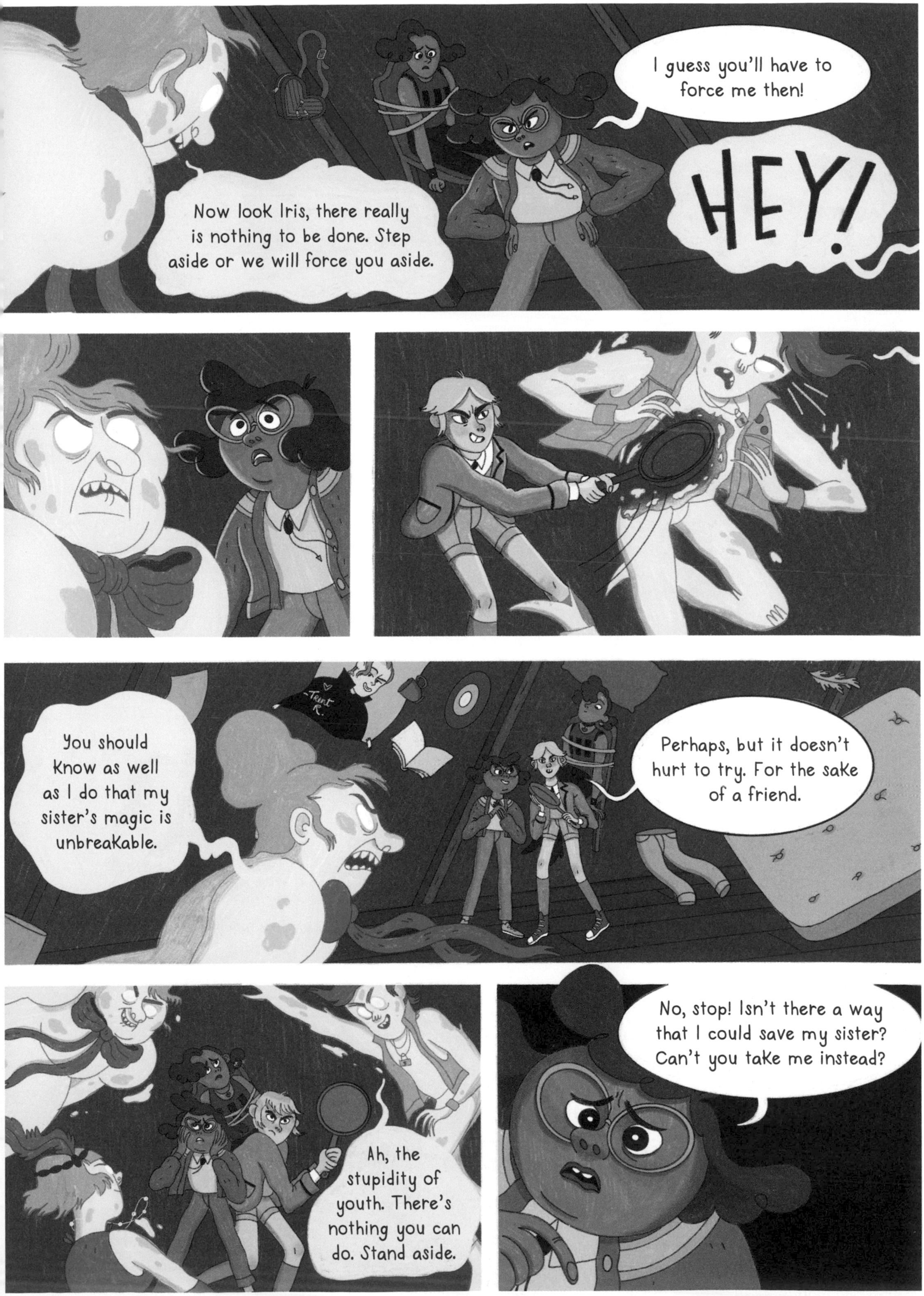

Now look Iris, there really is nothing to be done. Step aside or we will force you aside.
I guess you'll have to force me then!
HEY!
You should know as well as I do that my sister's magic is unbreakable.
Perhaps, but it doesn't hurt to try. For the sake of a friend.
Trent R.
Ah, the stupidity of youth. There's nothing you can do. Stand aside.
No, stop! Isn't there a way that I could save my sister? Can't you take me instead?

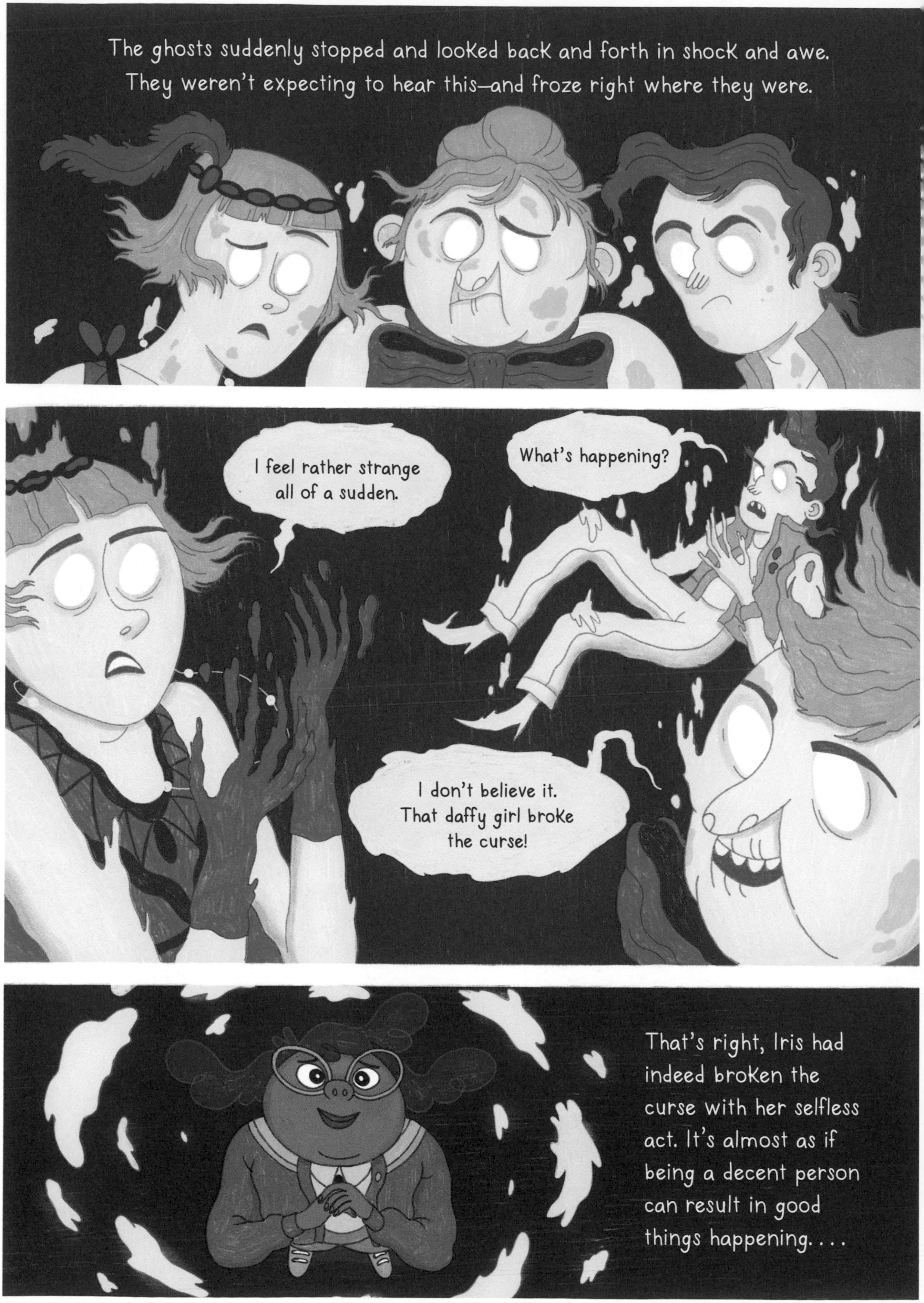
The ghosts suddenly stopped and looked back and forth in shock and awe. They weren't expecting to hear this—and froze right where they were.
I feel rather strange all of a sudden.
What's happening?
I don't believe it. That daffy girl broke the curse!
That's right, Iris had indeed broken the curse with her selfless act. It's almost as if being a decent person can result in good things happening. . . .

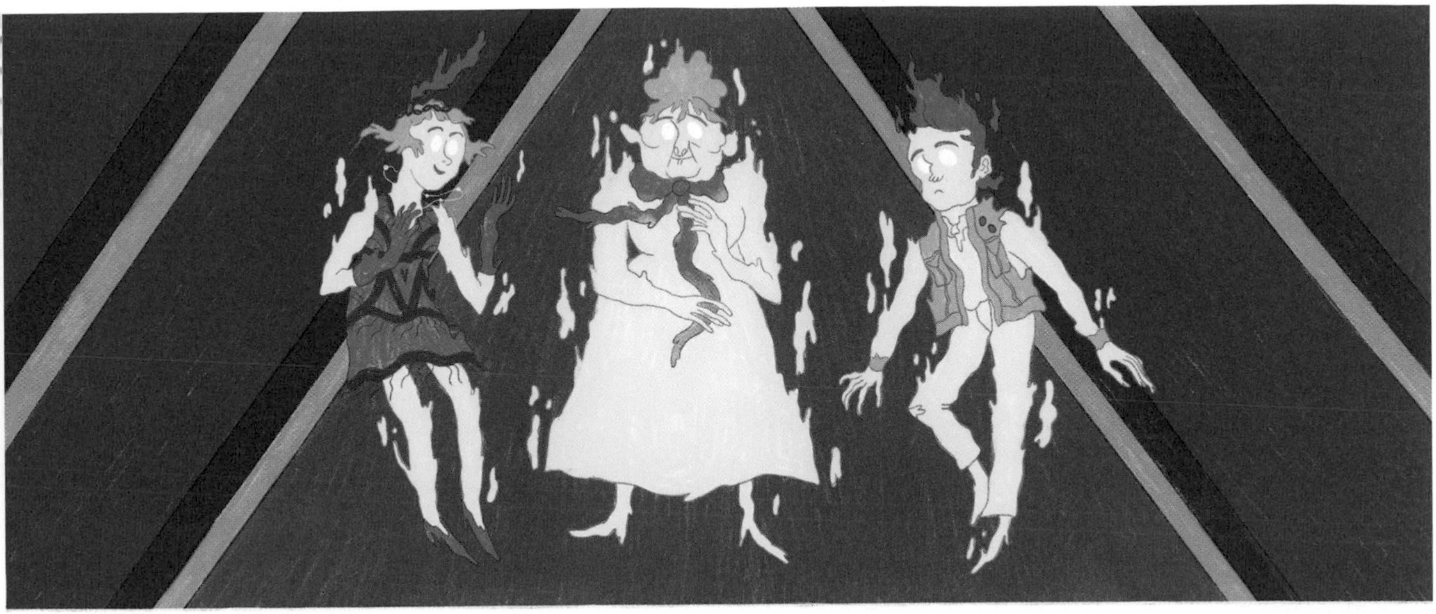

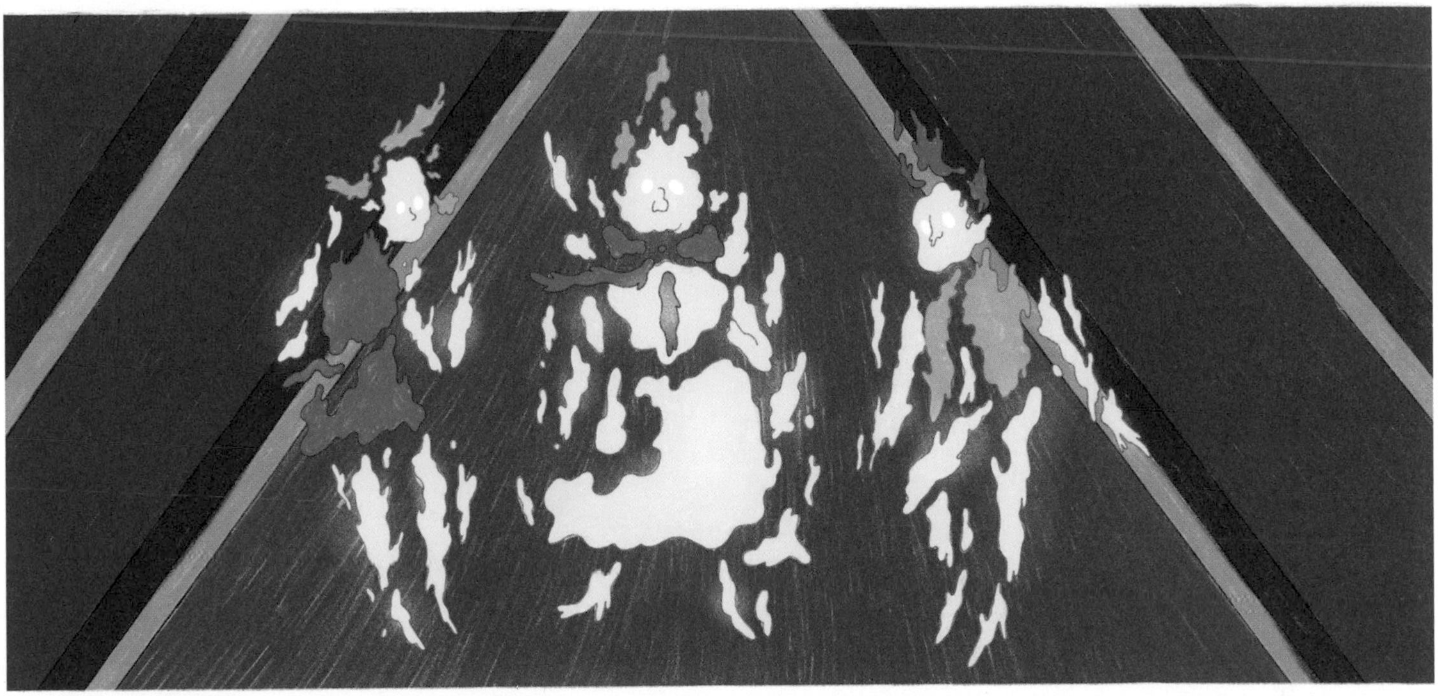

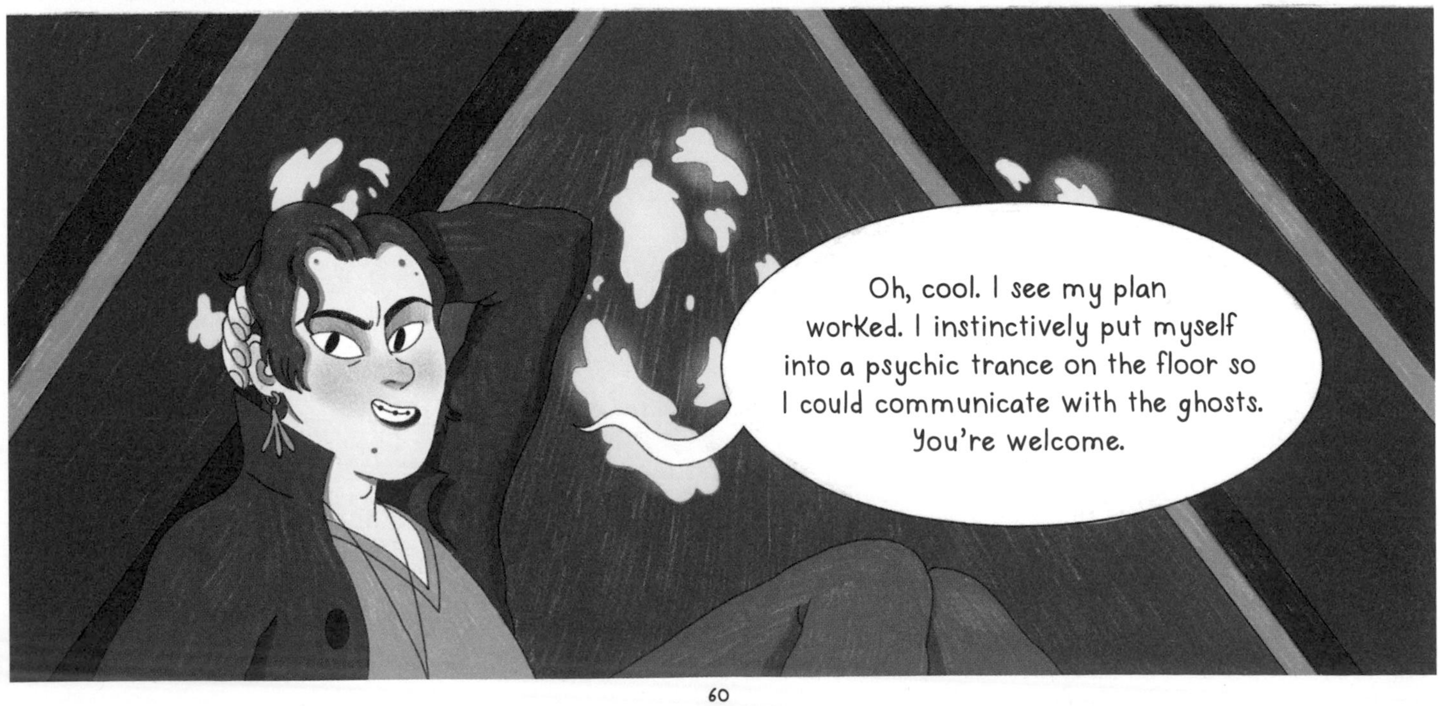

Oh, cool. I see my plan worked. I instinctively put myself into a psychic trance on the floor so I could communicate with the ghosts. You're welcome.

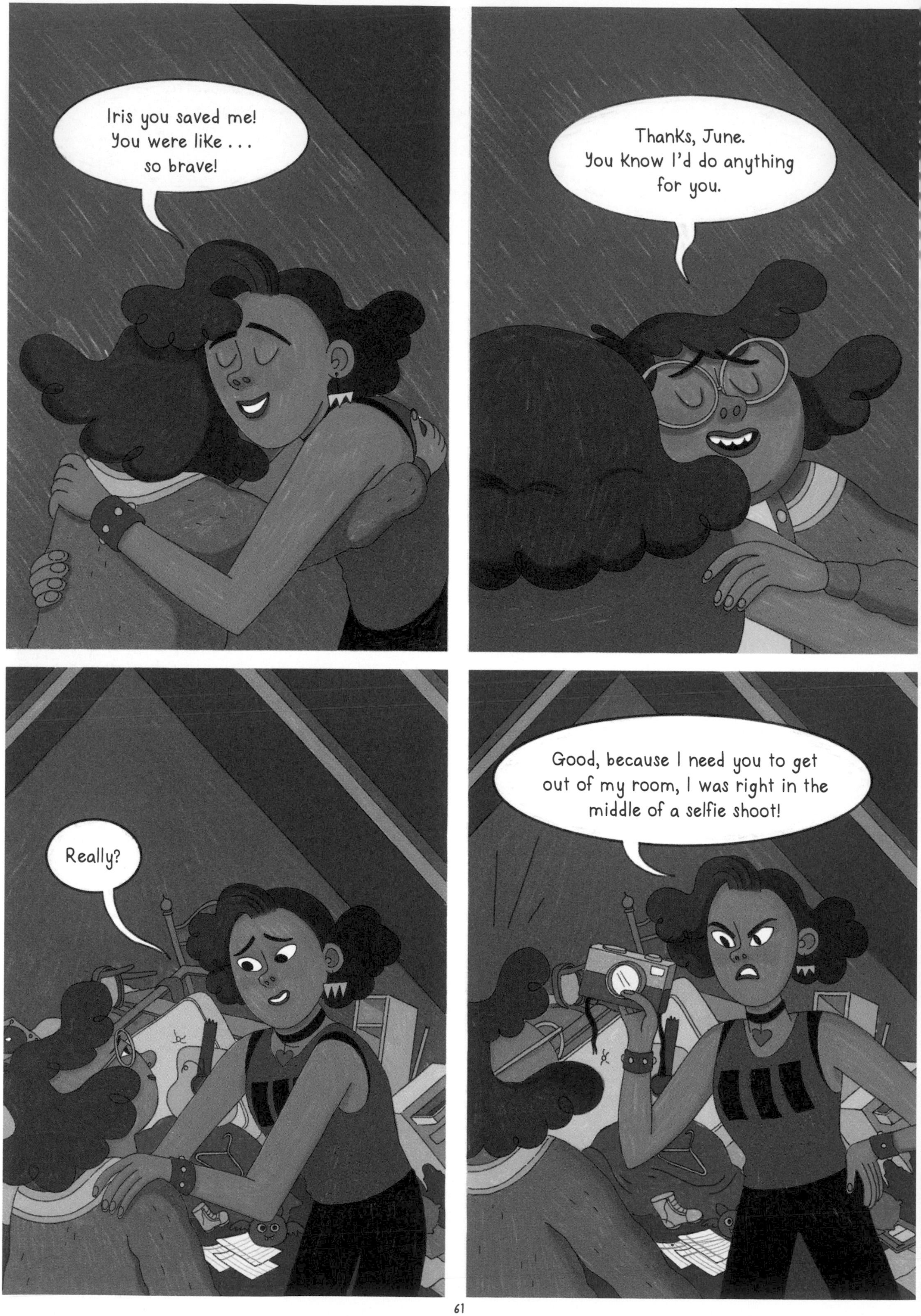
Iris you saved me! You were like . . . so brave!
Thanks, June. You know I'd do anything for you.
Really?
Good, because I need you to get out of my room, I was right in the middle of a selfie shoot!

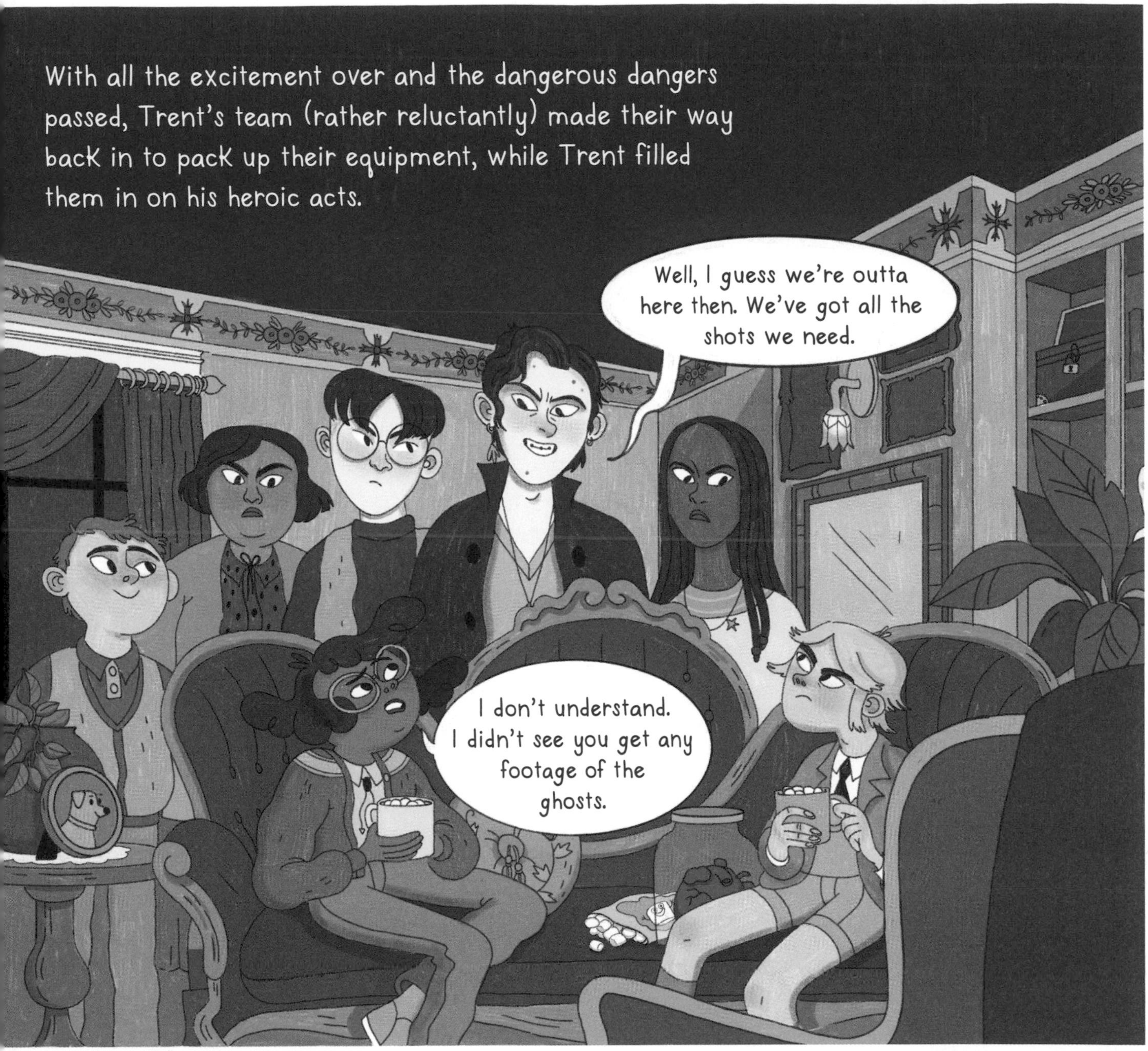
With all the excitement over and the dangerous dangers passed, Trent's team (rather reluctantly) made their way back in to pack up their equipment, while Trent filled them in on his heroic acts.
Well, I guess we're outta here then. We've got all the shots we need.
I don't understand. I didn't see you get any footage of the ghosts.

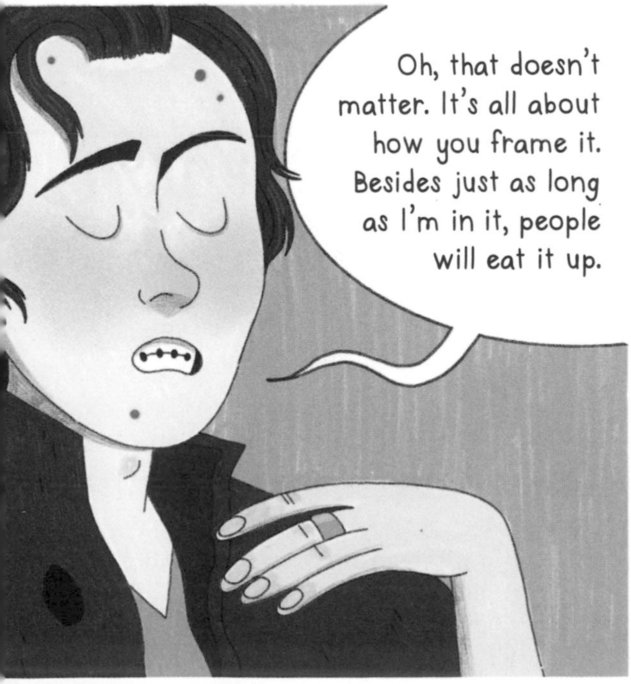
Oh, that doesn't matter. It's all about how you frame it. Besides just as long as I'm in it, people will eat it up.

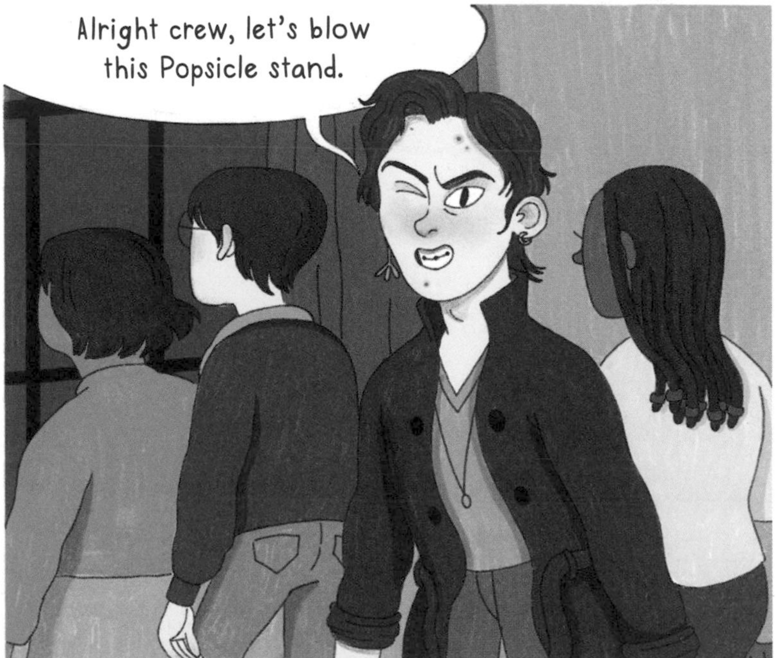
Alright crew, let's blow this Popsicle stand.

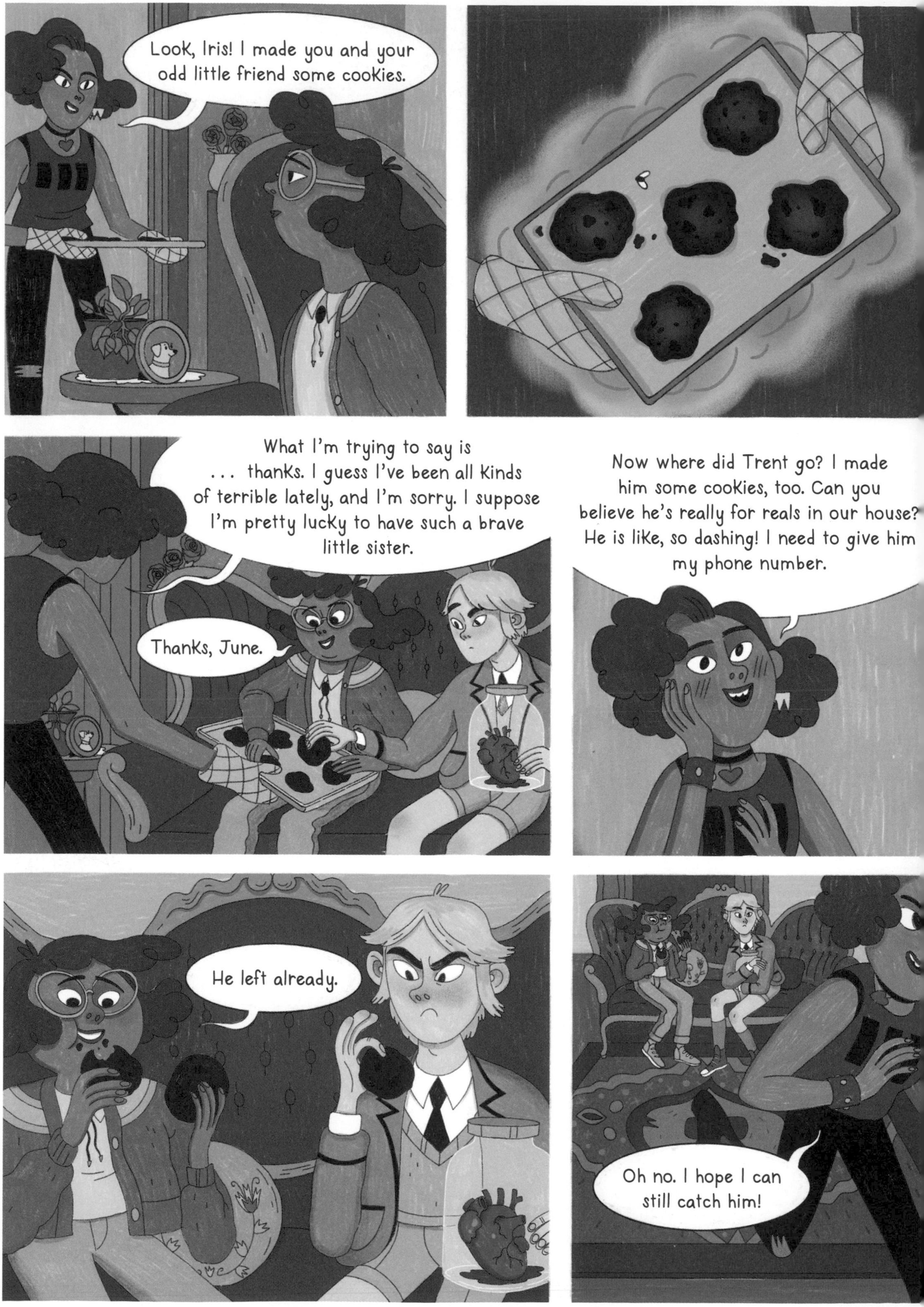
Look, Iris! I made you and your odd little friend some cookies.
What I'm trying to say is . . . thanks. I guess I've been all kinds of terrible lately, and I'm sorry. I suppose I'm pretty lucky to have such a brave little sister.
Thanks, June.
Now where did Trent go? I made him some cookies, too. Can you believe he's really for reals in our house? He is like, so dashing! I need to give him my phone number.
He left already.
Oh no. I hope I can still catch him!

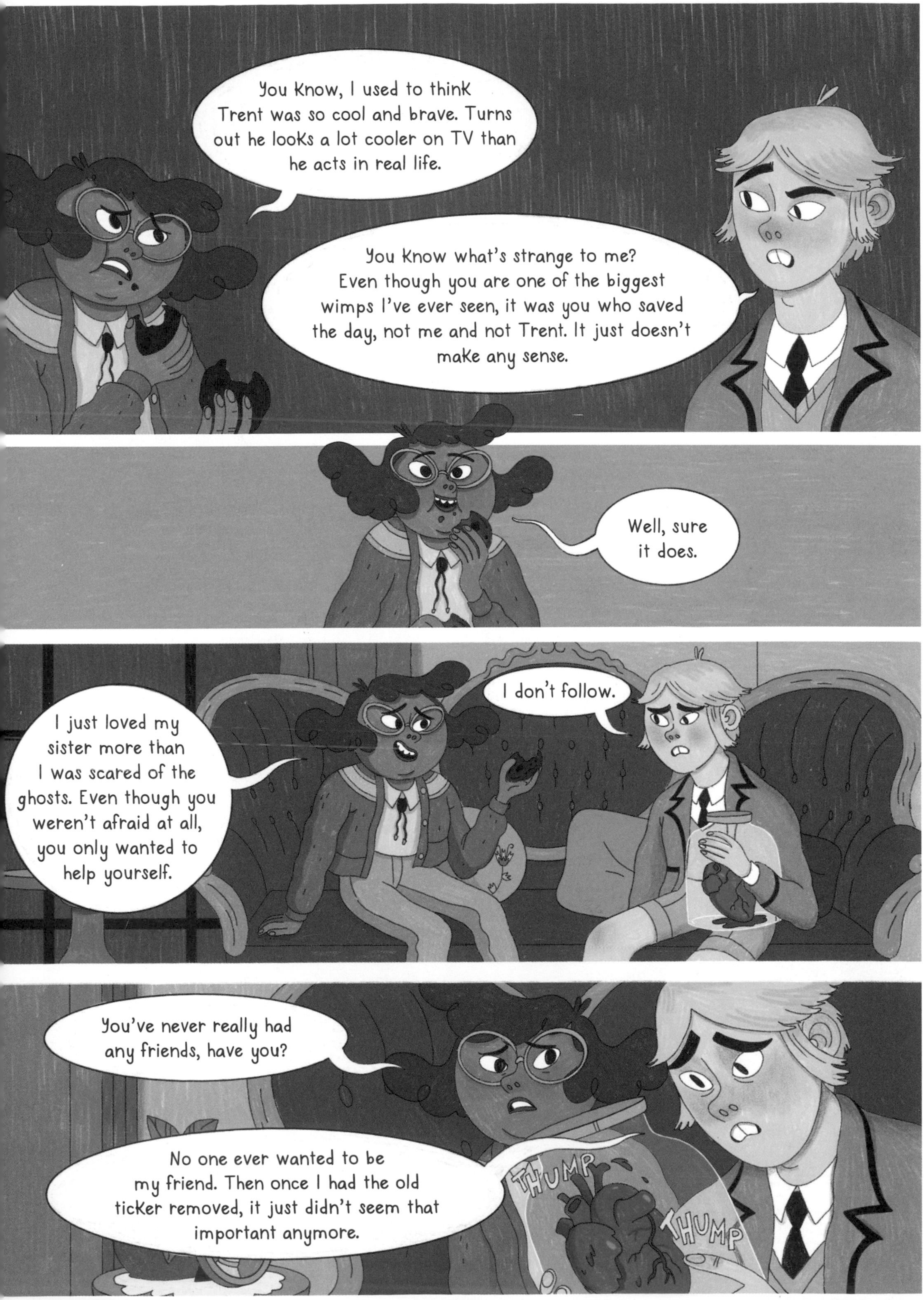
You know, I used to think Trent was so cool and brave. Turns out he looks a lot cooler on TV than he acts in real life.
You know what's strange to me? Even though you are one of the biggest wimps I've ever seen, it was you who saved the day, not me and not Trent. It just doesn't make any sense.
Well, sure it does.
I don't follow.
I just loved my sister more than I was scared of the ghosts. Even though you weren't afraid at all, you only wanted to help yourself.
You've never really had any friends, have you?
No one ever wanted to be my friend. Then once I had the old ticker removed, it just didn't seem that important anymore.
THUMP
THUMP

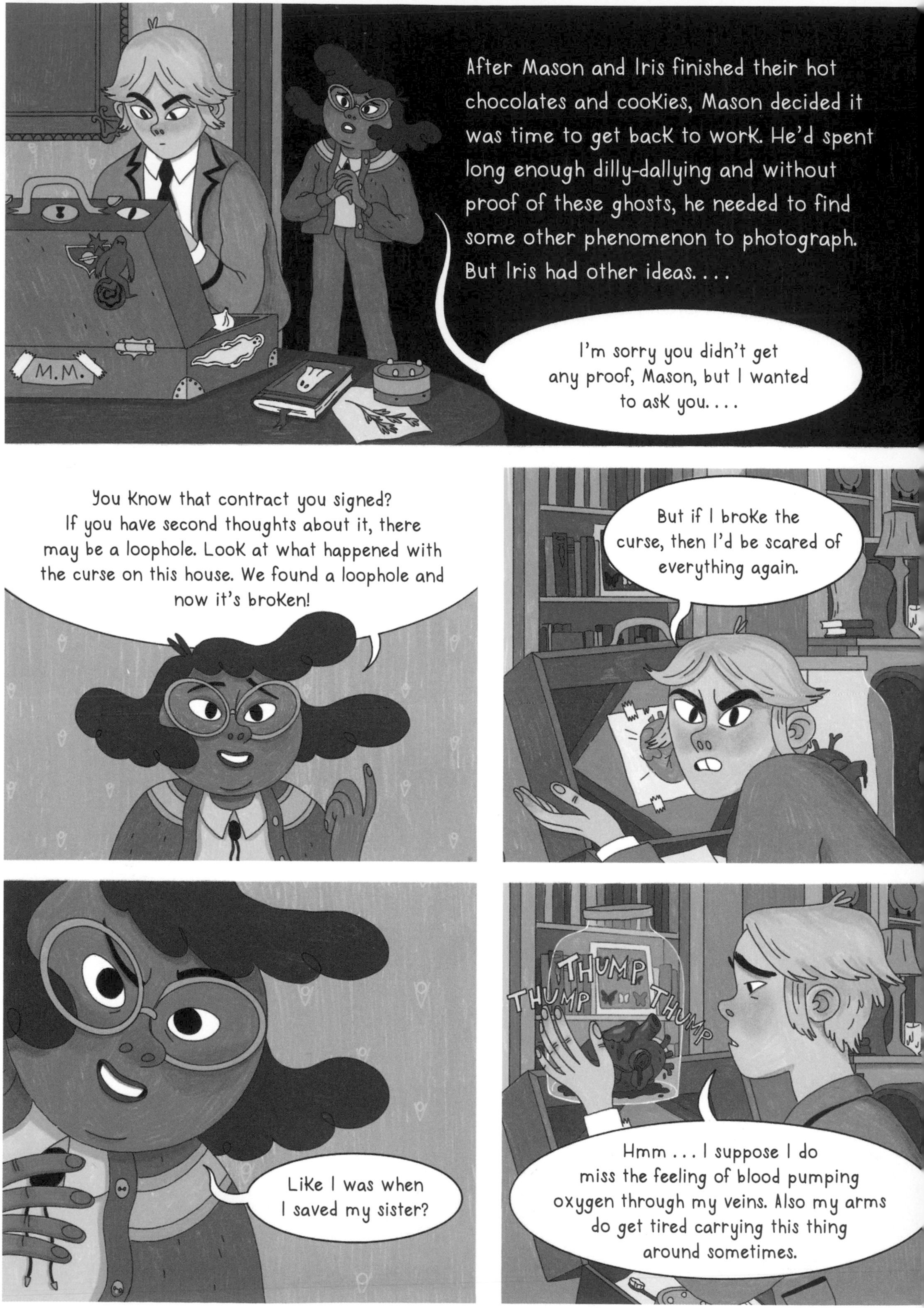
After Mason and Iris finished their hot chocolates and cookies, Mason decided it was time to get back to work. He'd spent long enough dilly-dallying and without proof of these ghosts, he needed to find some other phenomenon to photograph. But Iris had other ideas. . . .
M.M.
I'm sorry you didn't get any proof, Mason, but I wanted to ask you. . . .
You know that contract you signed? If you have second thoughts about it, there may be a loophole. Look at what happened with the curse on this house. We found a loophole and now it's broken!
But if I broke the curse, then I'd be scared of everything again.
Like I was when I saved my sister?
THUMP
THUMP
THUMP
Hmm . . . I suppose I do miss the feeling of blood pumping oxygen through my veins. Also my arms do get tired carrying this thing around sometimes.

I guess I could just glance at the contract again.

What's that fine print there?

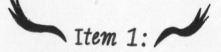

Reversal of curse may only be acknowledged and applied if the above signed successfully acquires the following items and returns them to the cursing party. The list consists of the following in full and no substitutions will be permitted.

Item 1:

Simple! If I know anything about witches' contracts—

And clearly you don't.

And clearly, I do! Then this means I've merely got to gather these items and Talitha will lift the curse.

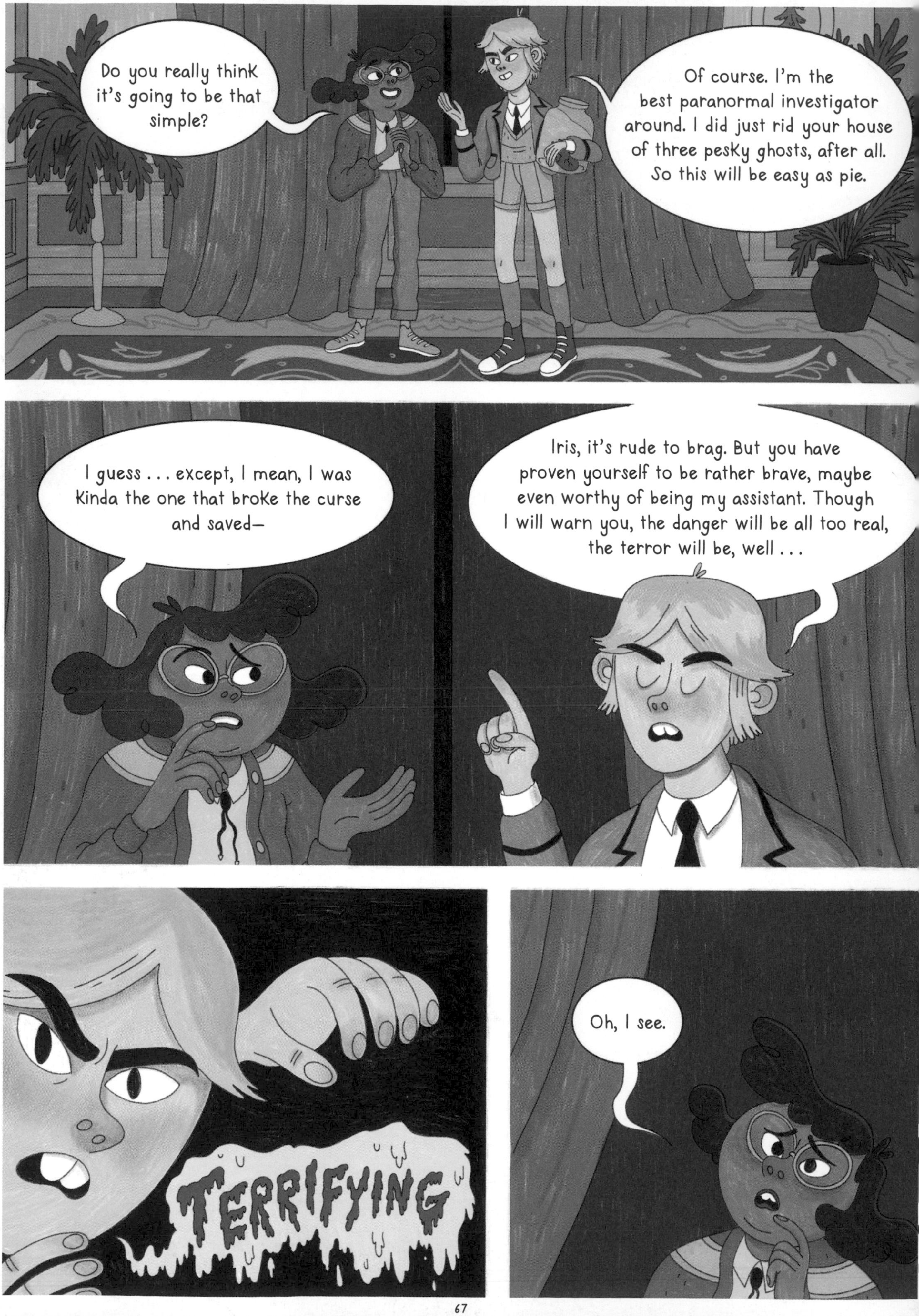
Do you really think it's going to be that simple?
Of course. I'm the best paranormal investigator around. I did just rid your house of three pesky ghosts, after all. So this will be easy as pie.
I guess . . . except, I mean, I was kinda the one that broke the curse and saved—
Iris, it's rude to brag. But you have proven yourself to be rather brave, maybe even worthy of being my assistant. Though I will warn you, the danger will be all too real, the terror will be, well . . .
TERRIFYING
Oh, I see.

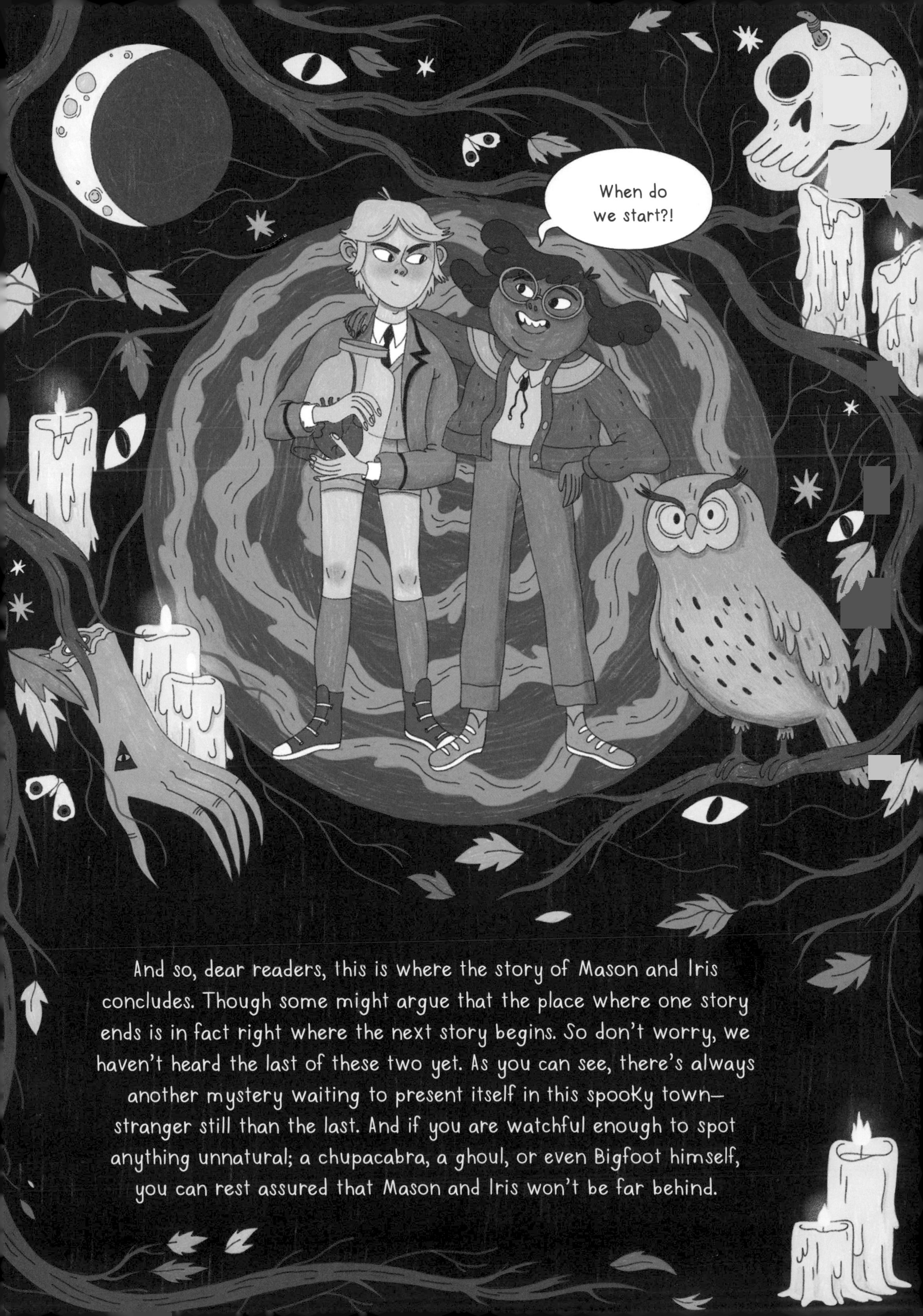
When do we start?!

And so, dear readers, this is where the story of Mason and Iris concludes. Though some might argue that the place where one story ends is in fact right where the next story begins. So don't worry, we haven't heard the last of these two yet. As you can see, there's always another mystery waiting to present itself in this spooky town—stranger still than the last. And if you are watchful enough to spot anything unnatural; a chupacabra, a ghoul, or even Bigfoot himself, you can rest assured that Mason and Iris won't be far behind.

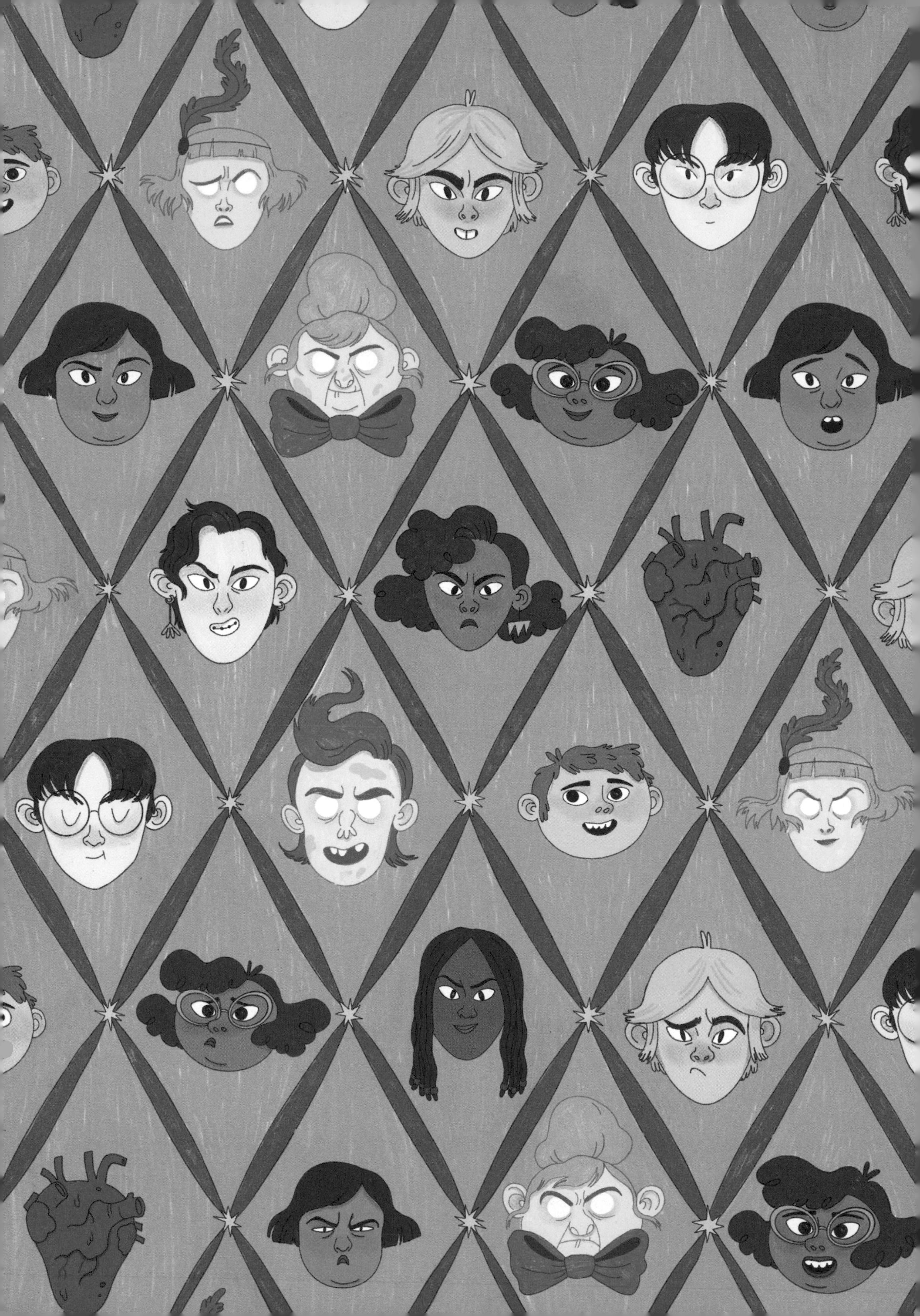